TROUBLE WAS A WOMAN

She came to Ruff in the night, and her warm body against his was enough to start the blood racing through his veins. She was soft, and her thigh was a warm miracle against his leg, her breasts round and firm, demanding attentive caresses. Her lips were gentle and pliant, finding his mouth and searching it diligently, each gentle touch stirring him more.

Her name was Abigail. She was another man's wife. She had been God only knew how many other men's woman. And from the moment Ruff laid eyes on her lush beauty and watched her running over him appraisingly, invitingly, he knew she was trouble.

But right now, even on a vengeance trail where a wrong move meant death, she was the kind of trouble that Ruff couldn't stay out of. . . .

Dark Angel Riding

Wild Westerns From SIGNET

RUFF JUSTICE #7

Dark Angel Riding

by
Warren T. Longtree

A SIGNET BOOK
NEW AMERICAN LIBRARY
TIMES MIRROR

Copyright © 1982 by The New American Library, Inc.

The first chapter in this book appeared in *The Spirit Woman War,* the sixth volume of this series.

SIGNET TRADEMARK REG. U.S. PAT. OFF. AND FOREIGN COUNTRIES REGISTERED TRADEMARK—MARCA REGISTRADA
HECHO EN CHICAGO, U.S.A.

SIGNET, SIGNET CLASSICS, MENTOR, PLUME, MERIDIAN AND NAL Books are published by The New American Library, Inc., 1633 Broadway, New York, New York 10019

First Printing, November, 1982

1 2 3 4 5 6 7 8 9

PRINTED IN THE UNITED STATES OF AMERICA

RUFF JUSTICE

He knew the West better than any man alive—a hostile, savage land rife with both violent outlaws and courageous adventurers. But Ruff Justice had a sixth sense that kept him breathing and saw his enemies dead. A scout for the U.S. Cavalry, he was paid to protect the public, and nobody was faster at sniffing out a killer, a crook, a con man—red or white, at close range or far. Anyone on the wrong side of the law would have to reckon with the menace of Ruff's murderously sharp stag-handled bowie knife, with his Colt pistol, and the Spencer rifle he cradled in his arms.

Ruff Justice, gentleman and frontier philosopher—good men respected him, bad men feared him, and women, good and bad, wanted him with all the wildness of the Old West.

1

THE SUN SLANTED through the ranks of tall, ancient pines. Molten pools of sunlight painted the forest floor. It was still early morning, the trees glistening with dew, the deep pine scent rich and pervasive. Red squirrels bounded from branch to branch and at the creek a doe stood stock still, water dripping from her muzzle like rivulets of mercury. The deer heard something, scented something not to its liking, and with three long bounds it was across the creek and into the blue-green forest.

Up the slope of the mountain, three hundred yards from the creek along an old trail smoothed by the moccasioned feet of the Shoshone, all those years ago when they had lived in these mountains, there stood a low log cabin. The roof was sod and the grass on it had begun to grow. It was bright green and appealing. There were even a dozen black-eyed susans sprouting just over the eaves.

There were no windows in the cabin, built by the trapper Monk McCall, who had lost his beaver pelts and his life in a rigged faro game in Laramie one spring and had never returned to the mountains or his tiny cabin.

There was a well-built native-stone chimney, gray and sloping. From it a thin tendril of smoke rose, sketching a wavering curlicue against the bright sky above the ancient pines.

Within there was a puncheon table, two chairs, a low

bed, a storeroom, and a big copper kettle where venison stew was boiling at this early hour—hence the smoke.

She was warm and close in the morning, and her blond hair was a pleasant tangle. Her green eyes were upon him, and he watched as she bent low, her breasts grazing his bare chest, and kissed him.

"You'll make me a lazy man yet," Ruff Justice complained.

"Why? If you wanted to get up you would," Louise told him.

"I should. There's a lot to do." She kissed his throat, the point of his chin, his ear, pausing there to whisper love words. "Horses need feed."

"The bay's getting fat anyway," Louise replied. "They're both lazy and woolly."

There were other arguments, but Ruff had forgotten what they were. Her lips were silky and moist against his. He ran his hands down the delicate curve of her spine and up the flaring sweep of her smooth buttocks, holding her to him as her kisses became more eager, as his own need stirred.

She had straddled him now as he lay on his back in the early morning. She smiled down at him, tossed back her long blond hair, and sat up, positioning herself until they fell together like two pieces of a puzzle and Ruff felt her warm welcoming body close around him.

"Sit still a minute, will you?" he asked.

"Like it?"

"What do you think?" His hands cupped her breasts, marveled at their smooth firmness, toyed with the pink buds which stood taut and eager. She smiled again and moved her hips slightly, inflaming him.

"That's not sitting still," he objected.

"No. I lied."

"You're a treacherous woman," he said. She continued to sway against him, her hips searching for that pagan rhythm, that ancient cadence of the flesh.

"Lascivious, hungry, wanton, bawdy," she agreed, punctuating each word with a thrust of her pelvis. Ruff's fingers toyed with the pale-blond bush which flourished between her legs.

"A woman after my own heart," he replied. His hands rested on her thighs, and he lay back, contributing nothing.

She was restless searcher, a swaying, joyous creature. Her hips rolled and her pelvis bucked against him in short, sudden spasms.

"It's been there waiting for you for so long. There was no one for so long," she said. Her voice was cadenced, matching her body's steady rhythm. Ruff glanced up at her face, now set in concentration. She frowned slightly as she sought the perfect spot, found it, and encouraged her body. Her eyes, green as emeralds, were closed now, her broad mouth set into a straight line.

She was a woman back from the dead, throwing herself hungrily into life's enjoyment. It wasn't just the sex that she loved. It was the forest and all of the small creatures which lived there. The morning frost, the burble of the silver creek, the sudden thunder of a summer storm, the pleasant warmth of a crackling fire. She loved it all, appreciated it intensely.

She had been taken by the Cheyenne and held by them for seven long years. Dragged from camp to camp, humiliated, subdued, but not defeated, never defeated. Ruff had pulled her out of that situation, and it was his luck, not hers. He had found a woman who could look life in the eye and wink, who could face death and spit contemptuously, who could laugh and make love at once, who was tender and yet resilient and capable.

She was reaching a crest of sensation. Her head was thrown back; her eyes, half-open, looked at nothing. Unfocused, they reflected delight and pleasure. Her lips had parted, revealing even white teeth, the tip of her pink tongue.

He could feel the tremors between her thighs, feel her alter and grow moist within, and he reached out, drawing her to him. She kissed him and shuddered, and he arched

3

his back, joining her in the rhythm, two swimmers moving downstream in a turbulent, joyous river.

Ruff's head spun as his blood boiled through expanded vessels. His body was a pulsing, taut thing, eager, ready, and as he felt her tremble and quake, felt her teeth bite lightly against his shoulder, felt her kneading hands grip so tightly that her nails dug into his flesh, her hips stop their constant motion, heard the small, indefinable moan deep within her throat, he reached his own surging climax.

She lay on top of him still, administering tiny kisses to shoulders, neck, cheek, chest. Her hands tangled themselves in his long dark hair, her finger traced the line of his drooping black mustache, and she laughed. Laughed with a depth of pleasure incredible to Ruff, and he asked, "Am I responsible for all of that?"

"Just you. No one else."

"Makes a man proud."

"I told you how it would be." She kissed him again and yawned. He grinned.

"Now who's lazy?"

"I've put in a hard day's work already," she answered. "I've done my morning chore."

"Chore, is it?" he asked, grabbing her shoulder, wrestling her teasingly down.

"Only an expression, you know. Am I getting better?"

"You couldn't get any better." He kissed her throat through the soft tangle of her pale hair and said, "I guess we really should get up. Today will be like yesterday if we don't."

"What was the matter with yesterday?"

"Nothing. But a man can't spend all day every day in bed. Makes him fat and lazy."

"I'll keep you trimmed down."

"To skin and bones." He poked a finger into her ribs. "Up, dammit, woman. Your man's hungry and the horses need tending."

She sat up, yawning again, rumpling her hair as Ruff slipped from the bed and put his pants on. Looking back

4

toward the bed and seeing her breasts full and inviting, he felt like crawling back in, like wasting another day in languorous lovemaking. She caught the expression in his eyes and laughed.

"The horses."

"The horses," he agreed. He had no intention of riding anywhere. The horses seemed a luxury at times. When they wanted to exercise, they walked, sometimes taking a picnic basket to the grassy, columbine-strewn park high on the mountainside. There they spent many an afternoon lazing in the sun, making love.

There were no longer any Indians in these mountains, and not another living soul for many miles. The nearest town was Deadwood, and Louise, her aristocratic impulses returning, insisted that Deadwood was not a town at all, but a scab on the wilderness, waiting the cleansing wind which would blow it away and into deserved oblivion. Ruff had to agree. It was a squat, ugly town, weathered and temporary by design. The gold seekers, boomtowners, gamblers, and whores ran the town. It was their sort of place: blistered by prairie suns, discolored by weather, dank, dreary, and deserving of death.

Ruff went to the stew pot, stirred it and tasted the venison. Still tough. That buck must have run up and down these slopes every day of his life, his muscles turning to leather.

Louise was beside him, wearing only an apron. She had her hands on her hips. Seeing the dry expression on Ruff's face she smiled.

"I told you it ought to be vegetable stew."

"It'll do. A man needs meat . . . to keep his strength up."

That prompted her to ask, "How is that shoulder, really?"

"Really, it's fine."

She looked at it, touching the star-shaped scars with her fingers. "Really?" It still looked very nasty. It was too red, she thought. Ruff had taken two bullets in that shoulder, and it had nearly killed him. You could still see the

5

concavity where chunks of meat were missing, blasted away.

"Really." He hugged her for a moment, tasting her hair. Actually it hurt like hell, and probably always would. He thought there were still chips of bone moving around in there. On cold mornings the shoulder was almost useless, but there was no point in telling her all that.

"Tend your horses," she said lightly, feeling his rising interest.

"I'd best. If I get my ambition back I'll shear that winter coat from the gray."

"If you get your ambition back, you come see me . . . later!" she laughed. "I'm going down to the creek for a bath."

Ruff went out first. Morning was crisp and bright. He noticed the raccoon tracks near the porch. He could see the silver mirror of the creek downslope. Besides that there was only deep forest, primeval and magnificent.

Stepping from the porch he went to the pole corral behind the house where the horses greeted him with eager muzzles. He patted Louise's bay and then his gray horse. He had picked the gray up from a mountain man who had found gold, seen the light, and was going to St. Louis to see how quickly he could die happy.

The horse was a deep-chested gelding, its tail black, its mane almost white. A splash of white decorated its left haunch. Ruff got the fork out of the lean-to toolshed and forked hay to the horses. He had cut the hay himself from one of the high meadows.

Looking back toward the house, he saw Louise walking toward the creek, her step light and bouncy. She must have felt his eyes on her, for she turned and waved before disappearing around a bend in the trail, vanishing into the deep blue-green spruce forest.

Ruff curried the gray, and then his shoulder began to act up and he put the curry comb up, deciding the trim job could wait for another day.

He was getting lazy. But he had the right. He had no work to do—the army had finally given him a shove out the door after the Spirit Woman war threat had faded out. He had a little money and a fine woman. There was a lot of game, a tight little cabin. He felt none of his old compulsions—the need to ride to somewhere, anywhere, to see what lay beyond the hills, the need to be involved in life's turbulence.

He couldn't remember ever having been so content. A woman will do that. He kept thinking it was probably temporary, waiting for the spell Louise cast to wear off. But it hadn't yet. Maybe it never would.

He put the fork away, patted the muzzle of the gray, and walked toward the creek, thinking how pleasurable it would be to watch Louise at her bath, a wood nymph in the quick-running creek.

He had gone halfway when he met her returning from her bath.

"What's the matter?" she laughed.

"Too late," Ruff said. He folded her into his arms, feeling her cool flesh beneath the thin cotton dress she wore. "I felt like a little peeping."

"It's too darn cold," she said. "The snow must be melting up above." She put on a sly expression. "Come up to the house. I'll show you whatever you like."

Ruff held her to him, kissed her eyebrows, her nose, and her lips.

"Race you!" she said suddenly. She tore away from his arm, and with a laugh she started away. It was then that the shot rang out, and with the laugh still in her throat, Louise died.

She fell to the earth, and Ruff couldn't move. He couldn't accept it. It was not reality. It was a nightmare. She was there, laughing, alive. Then she had stepped around him, and simply crumpled up.

Her mouth was filled with blood, that tender, laughing mouth. There was a fist-sized hole through her breast. Something ugly, purple, protruded from her chest. Smoke rose from her dress in back.

Ruff was slow in reacting. Finally he threw himself to one side and dodged behind the base of a tree. He had his

Colt in his hand, although he couldn't remember drawing it. He searched the long hills, but saw no smoke. Maybe his attention wasn't sharp enough.

He couldn't keep his eyes from her. She lay there dead. *Dead*. But she couldn't be dead. She was laughing. She had been taking a bath. She was going to race him to the cabin, where they would indulge in love play.

She couldn't die just like that. It was a trick. She had decided to play a trick on him, to fill her mouth with something which looked like blood, to contrive a hole in her breast, to fool him, to make him laugh.

But she lay sprawled against the earth, her mouth open, those emerald eyes open to the sky. A jay squawked and Ruff wanted to kill it. That was what he wanted more than anything in the world. To kill something so that Louise could come back to life.

There were no more shots. He couldn't get a handle on reality. He had lived with death all of his adult years, but this was different. She was taking a bath. She was going to race him to the cabin. He had seen her hoist her skirt, seen her laugh.

And in that moment she had stepped around Ruff and taken a bullet which was surely meant for him.

He moved swiftly and quietly through the forest, his mind a red blur. Throughout most of the morning he searched the woods, moving like a ghost, a shadow. His Colt became a part of him, an extension of his wish to kill. He did not think, reason. He simply searched. If he thought, he knew that his thoughts would return to the woman below, the one who lay sprawled against the meadow.

He was a beast, a specter, a killing thing which thought no more than an angered grizzly.

When, shortly after noon when the mocking sun rode high in a crystal sky, he found the tracks, found the bright casing, the man was long gone. His horse had left only a few indistinct tracks across the pineneedle-littered earth, but Ruff found three cigarette butts and a partial print. He had ridden a horse with a chipped shoe on the

8

right hind foot. He smoked wheatstraw cigarettes. He used a .56 Spencer rifle. A rifle designed for buffalo. A rifle which could blow a cavernous hole in a young woman's chest, revealing purple secrets.

What he did with the rest of the afternoon he didn't know. It was all a nightmare, unreal. Twice he went to the cabin, thinking she would be there, laughing, her head cocked to one side, her hands on her lovely hips, asking where he had been.

But she was not there. She was in the meadow, growing cold against the earth.

He buried her at dusk, beneath a massive broken cedar, covering the grave with cold, rich earth and pine needles. You couldn't tell anyone was buried there. It was a smooth and level grave. She had never been.

He had no compulsion to put up a marker, to carve her name in the cedar. He simply stood, watching dusk purple the skies, watching the earth grow colder.

Later he walked through the twilight to the corral. He looked at her bay horse a long while, recalling the pleasure she had had in riding it, recalling the maverick way the horse had nipped at her legs each morning as she mounted it.

He turned the bay loose, slamming his fist against its haunch to get it running. There was grass in the high country.

Then he saddled his gray and walked it to the cabin. When he went in the scent of venison stew, the scent of Louise, met him. He looked at the rumpled bed, and then he knew what he must do.

He took a burning brand from the fire and touched it to the bed until it smoldered and burst into flame. He set fire to the curtains she had made with material brought from Deadwood that fall morning. Then he turned and went from the cabin.

He rode out without looking back to watch as flames devoured the cabin, as golden sparks rose into the night sky.

He halted the gray at the edge of the meadow and

looked out over the black forest, the empty flatlands beyond. He would find him. Find this monster with the big buffalo gun. He would find him if he had to cross deserts or mountains in winter. He would find him if it took a lifetime. If he had to drag himself after the killer on bloody stumps until he could cut the life from him.

He would find him and the man would die painfully, slowly, knowing that it was Ruff Justice who had done it.

He would be running now. He could run, but he couldn't hide.

He could try to hide, bury himself in wilderness dens or lose himself in some big city. But he couldn't avoid the retribution Ruff Justice would deal out.

The killer was a beast, a savage murderer who had cut the world out from under Ruff Justice's feet. He was a coward, a mongrel bastard, an evil, stinking vermin awaiting vengeance. And Ruff Justice was vengeance, the hand of retribution, a dark angel riding.

He heeled the big gray and rode down through the deep, empty forest.

2

CORPORAL WYATT HORNE was one of the two men on gate guard. From his perch on the palisade he could see the Missouri, ice-blue, flowing southward past Fort Lincoln. There were oak and willow along the river, and plenty of trout beneath the surface. Horne was a fisherman through and through. If there were any way a man could make a living taking trout from those shady pools he knew of, Horne would have left army service in a minute. Thrown down his carbine, deserted if he had to. No way had yet been devised for a trout fisherman to make his living at it, however; Horne had to content himself with using off-duty hours to deceive the rainbows.

He made his turn at the end of the parapet and had a view of Bismarck, the town which had sprung up only a stone's throw away from Fort Abraham Lincoln, Dakota Territory. It wasn't a lot of town, but it was growing—haphazardly, Horne thought, with shacks thrown up at the outskirts, with new downtown buildings made of old lumber going up randomly. Saloons—two thirds of them were saloons. The town marshal, Tom Dukes, had his hands full.

Those who had swarmed into the territory with the opening of the Black Hills to gold seekers had rushed back out of the hills recently. They had good reason. Red Cloud was raising pure hell out there. And so the prospectors, tinhorns, card sharpers, soiled women, pick-pockets, and speculators were holed up in Bismarck. Now and again the army had to ride over and put down an overexuberant celebration. Even Tom Dukes, late of Abilene, had his limitations.

Not that One-Eye wasn't tough. He was pure mean and had no aversion to putting a slug in a man's belly if that was what it took to slow him down. Usually that was just what it took. These latecomers—General Crook had termed them "border ruffians," this edge of Dakota being properly the U.S. territorial border as of now—all seemed to be three sizes bigger than the men back East. At least they thought they were. They were all hair and horns, apt to sprout steel when irritated. They were frequently irritated.

The damned fools had brought trouble with them. They had gone into the Black Hills, angered the Sioux and Cheyenne beyond endurance, and then come hightailing it back to Bismarck, screaming for the army to make the hills safe. They wouldn't be safe for a while yet, a long while.

Horne turned again, shifting his rifle to the other shoulder, manual recommendations aside. Then he paused. Squinting into the bright April sunlight, he saw the lone rider coming in. His horse was a tall rangy gray with a black tail and a white mane. An unusual-looking animal, and a lot of horseflesh.

Horne shaded his eyes with his hand and looked again, intently, at the rider. Slowly he cursed, grinning simultaneously.

"Never thought to see you again. Not after last time," Horne said to the still distant figure.

He was clad in buckskins. He wore a black hat with an extremely broad brim and had a red scarf tied around the crown of his hat. He wore his black hair long. Across his saddle bows he carried a rifle sheathed in a fringed buckskin scabbard.

Horne was still smiling. This was too good to keep to himself. He called to Lloyd Burke, who was at the far corner of the front parapet. Burke, PFC, Lloyd D. cupped a hand to his ear and shouted something.

"Come here!" Corporal Horne waved a beckoning arm, and Burke, glancing down at the parade ground, not seeing that bastard Holderlin, the watch sergeant, ambled over to where Horne stood.

"What is it?"

"Look, man." Horne turned the private by his shoulders. "Look right there."

"The civilian?"

"Yes, dammit. Don't you know who that is, for Christ's sake? That, Private Burke, is Mr. Ruffin T. Justice."

Burke's gaze took on fresh alertness. He peered with sharp interest at the incoming rider. "You sure?" Burke asked almost in a whisper.

"Sure I am. You wait and see!"

"Are you forgetting, Horne?" the PFC said.

"Forgetting . . . ?"

"The damned order. The *persona non grata* order."

The grin fell away from Horne's face. He had forgotten. It had sent them all scurrying to discover what *persona non grata* meant. That Lieutenant Paulsen had drafted the order for the colonel, and Paulsen always seemed to be doing his best to make things obscure. They had simply started calling the order the Ruff Justice Regulation.

It read that those civilians deemed unacceptable should no longer be given access to Fort Lincoln or any of its amenities. They hadn't known what "amenities" meant either. What the order meant now was that Horne was going to have to tell Ruff Justice that he wasn't allowed on the property. It was enough to erase anyone's good spirits.

"Come on," Horne said. "Burke!"

"I thought you could handle it," Burke lied. He didn't want to be near the powder keg when it went up any more than Horne did.

Horne, climbing down the pole ladder and walking to the open gate, could now see Justice's face in the shadow of that wide-brimmed hat, which flopped and twisted with the wind's whimsy. The face was lean and purposeful. The eyes, blue and set, stared out coldly at the world. There was none of the humor Horne had always associated with the man in those eyes. His expression was damned near wolfish, and Horne felt a shiver crawl along his spine.

Ruff was within twenty feet of the gate when Horne stepped out and blocked his entry, his rifle held at an angle across his chest. From the corner of his eye Horne saw Burke coming slowly forward to side him, but you'd think the man's feet were made of lead.

"Hello, Wyatt," Ruff Justice said, reining in that gray horse.

"Hello, Ruff," Horne answered hesitantly. Justice's voice seemed to come from a great distance. It was hard and cold, scarcely human. Something had happened, something black and bloody—Horne decided he did not want to know what it was.

"You want to let me in?" Ruff asked, his eyes lifting momentarily to the parade ground where Indians, horse traders, immigrants, farmers, drilling soldiers, and fur trappers intermingled indiscriminately.

"Well . . ." Horne swallowed hard. "Thing is, Mr. Justice—Ruff—we've been told not to let you in. There's a list of men who aren't exactly in favor with the colonel, you see, and orders are not to let none of them on post."

"Wyatt," Ruff said, leaning forward, "I am going to come onto this post. What I'm asking is if you'll please step aside and make it easier for me, and for yourself," he added unnecessarily.

Wyatt Horne found that his mouth had gone suddenly dry. He could hear the blood racing in his ears. It irked him, for Wyatt Horne was far from being a coward. It angered him only because it was Ruff Justice he had to face down, and he couldn't do it. What was the worst they could do to him? he wondered. Take his stripes. Hell, if it hadn't been for Ruff back there at Dirty Tanks, he wouldn't even be alive. Stripes came and they went.

"Lloyd," Corporal Horne said, "I think you'd best return to your post."

"Corporal . . ." Burke started to object. "I'm with you."

"No you're not. You're on the parapet. Anything happens, you don't know anything about it. Get on back up there."

Burke hesitated for a second, but then he turned sharply on his heel and marched off. Horne watched him for a moment, then with a wan smile he stepped aside and let Justice onto the post.

Ruff nodded his appreciation. Those blue eyes were as cold as ever, his mouth still determined, and with a little sigh of relief Horne watched him ride onto the parade ground.

"That was no mistake," Horne told himself. "He was coming on one way or the other." Shrugging it off, Horne climbed back up the pole ladder to the parapet and started slowly walking his rounds, wondering how long it would be before Sergeant Holderlin showed up to blister his ears.

Ruff Justice rode his gray at a walk. Neither hand touched the reins—he guided the horse with the pressure of his knees as an Indian guides a good buffalo pony. His eyes, constantly moving, searched the throng.

Horses were being traded, Indian blankets and knives. There was a band of Crow Indians there trading furs. The sutler was hawking lemonade from a makeshift plank counter and, surprisingly, selling a lot of it. Dust billowed up from a passing freight wagon, sifting slowly down, veiling the post briefly.

The huge sergeant was waddling down the plankwalk, duty roster in his hand. It was warm, and First Sergeant Mack Pierce could feel the perspiration trickling down his neck. He paused to let a sod-buster woman and her brood of four pass. He dabbed at his throat with his handkerchief and started on, turning his head as a freight wagon, spuming dust, clattered toward the gate.

Abruptly Pierce stopped.

"Christ!" He barely whispered it. "I've got to be wrong," he told himself. But he wasn't. The tall man had turned his gray and was now headed directly away from Pierce. He could see nothing of his face, but then First Sergeant Mack Pierce didn't need to. There are men who couldn't hide their identity if they wanted to.

"Collins!" He grabbed a passing trooper by the arm and handed him the duty roster. "Post this for me." Then he stepped heavily from the plankwalk and set his vast bulk into reluctant motion.

Justice had spied the man he wanted, and he swung down. He strode toward the horse trader, his rifle in the crook of his arm, the gray trailing.

"What can I do for you?" the horse trader asked with good humor. He was white-haired, probably French, an old plains hand. He looked at Ruff Justice, still smiling until their eyes met. "What is it, friend?" he asked warily.

"I just want to look at your horses," Ruff said. The trader relaxed visibly.

Ruff moved forward, dropping the reins of his gray. The horse stood obediently in place. Justice walked around the roan gelding before him, resting a hand on the animal's haunch.

"Trot him around," the Frenchman invited. "Sound as a dollar."

Ruff ignored the man, lifted the right hind hoof, examined it briefly, and let go. He moved to a piebald mare and did the same, the horse trader in his tracks, extolling the virtues of the mare.

"Well?"

Justice looked him in the eye and said nothing. He was moving toward the next horse on the Frenchman's string, a blue roan with a black muzzle, when he heard the feet behind him. Turning, Ruff found himself face to face with Sergeant Mack Pierce. Behind Pierce were eight armed troopers.

"What is this?" Ruff asked.

Pierce looked the plainsman up and down. "It's an escort, Ruff. You're not allowed on post. Not after . . ."

Ruff ignored him, lifted the right hind leg of the blue roan, and, frowning, moved on to the next animal. Mack Pierce managed to get his considerable bulk between Justice and the broken-down bay.

"Move it, Mack."

"Can't do it, Ruff. It's orders."

"And you were always a stickler for orders."

"Most times."

"Get out of my way, Mack."

"Listen, Ruff. You were a good scout, *army*! What in hell's the matter with you?" Pierce's voice was taut with strain. Ruff growled an answer.

"Get the hell out of my way."

"Can't do it." Pierce, his monumental body quivering, shook his head sadly. "Not on my own authority. You want to see the major?"

"Major? Where's MacEnroe?"

"The colonel's on leave. Kansas City. Major Burnett's in command. You want to talk to him, or leave?"

"I won't leave until I'm finished," Ruff said. The roan tossed its head and snorted. The Frenchman had been slowly backing away as the troopers circled Ruff, their Springfields lowered.

"Ruff," Mack Pierce said, spreading his hands, "you see how it is."

"I see."

"What'll it be?"

"I don't seem to have a choice right now," Justice said.

Mack Pierce said, "No, I guess you don't."

Pierce started to reach for the long-barreled Colt at Ruff's hip, but there was something in those hard blue eyes which caused his hand to fall away. He turned to his troopers.

"I won't need you." He looked again at Ruff, who nodded his head. "Fall out."

The soldiers reluctantly drifted away as Mack Pierce led Ruff toward the orderly room. Another old friend, Ray Hardistein, was inside the building, but Ruff seemed hardly to notice him. With Pierce still at his elbow, they entered the major's office, Pierce rapping on the door-frame first to announce them.

Major Ralph Burnett, overaged for his grade, West Point class of '50, on his first tour of duty in the West, looked up as his first sergeant entered, escorting a tall, lean man in buckskins.

Burnett had seen his share of duty during "the War," under Sheridan and then under Grant himself. Since that time he had lain dormant in a Washington office, perfunctorily attending balls and War Department meetings alike, watching younger men ascend the hierarchy, those he considered less competent achieve greater rank. He was now a red-faced, balding man of forty-five who had seen no combat in twelve years, and who knew that coming west was his only chance to make field grade before retirement.

Burnett hated the West, hated the Indians, hated the lackadaisical army General Crook had allowed to develop in Dakota; hated the dust and the cold, the town of Bismarck, and the maverick civilians he had had to deal with since Colonel MacEnroe had departed for a month's furlough.

It looked like he had another one—the civilian before him now was a typical hardcase, rough, raw, unmovable. Burnett read it in his eyes. Unfortunately he didn't read the rest of the man's character there.

"Sir, beg pardon," Pierce said, saluting. "This here is Mr. Ruff Justice." He nodded at the lean, buckskinned man beside him.

Burnett flagged a slow salute toward Mack Pierce and let his eyes, with what he hoped was an intimidating glare, rest on Justice.

"What's he doing here, Sergeant Pierce?" Burnett opened a desk drawer and with a little shuffling found the infamous order. "He's on the top of this list."

"He hasn't said, sir—what he's doing here, that is," Mack Pierce replied, shifting his considerable weight to the other leg.

"Mr. Justice," the major began, "you are not welcome

18

on this post for reasons best known to you and Colonel MacEnroe. You are to leave immediately."

"I will, when I'm through with my business."

"You have no business here!" Burnett exploded.

"I do. I'll see to it and then I'll be on my way . . . maybe."

"Maybe?" Burnett sputtered a bit and came to his feet. "I don't know who you think you are, sir, but by God I'll have you—"

"Court-martialed?" Ruff suggested with a trace of a smile.

"Get him off this post," Burnett said, seating himself, waving a hand in a gesture of dismissal.

"Major, it won't be that easy." Ruff Justice leaned forward and rested his hands on the officer's desk. "I came here on private business. I won't be here long, I won't be interfering with army routine." He added thoughtfully, "Unless it's a soldier involved."

"Involved? Involved in what?"

"Murder."

"I don't see . . ."

"Someone tried to kill me. Instead he shot a woman I was with." He looked at Mack Pierce. "It was Louise, Mack. Some bastard shot her. She's dead."

"Have you reported this to the law?" Burnett's rigid mask was slightly askew; he seemed concerned now more than outraged.

"I don't want the law involved," Ruff said in a way which chilled Burnett.

"But why are you here?"

"I found his sign. He was riding a horse with a chipped right hind shoe. I tracked that horse, major. Tracked it right up to your front gate. Tracks lead in but they don't lead out."

"Are you saying one of my troopers did it?"

"No. I don't think so. I found the cartridge casing. It was from a .56 Spencer. Hardly army-issue. Could still be a soldier, but I don't think it is."

"You're looking for the horse, then," Major Burnett said, nodding his understanding.

"That's right. The horse and the man who rode him."

"And if you do find him?" Burnett's eyes narrowed. Ruff Justice only shrugged. "Look here, Justice, I can understand why you're here. It's a terrible thing, murdering a woman." He ran a harried hand across his thinning hair. "But I won't have you doing murder on this post." The major stood, turning to look out the window. "I'll make you a bargain—if he's a soldier, turn him over to me. If he's a civilian, we'll hold him for Tom Dukes. If he's gone, he's your meat."

"If I don't like this bargain?"

"Then, by God, I'll have ten good men in here and you'll be trundled off this post!"

Ruff smiled faintly again. What was going on behind those eyes Burnett couldn't have said. Finally he replied, "I'll take the bargain. I don't seem to have much choice."

"No." Burnett's face sagged with relief. As Justice was turning to go, the major asked, "By the way, just how did you get onto this post?"

"Over the back fence, major. You really ought to have a guard posted there."

"Over . . . ?" Justice had already turned and was striding toward the door to the major's office, rifle dangling from his hand. "Well, Pierce! Stay with him, man. Stay with him!"

Pierce spun around, saluting negligently, and ambled after Justice, grinning as he passed through the orderly room. Sergeant Ray Hardistein stood in the outer door, looking at Ruff's receding back.

"What's up, Mack?" he inquired.

"Grab your hat and your gun and you'll find out."

Hardistein did just that, following his wheezing first sergeant out into the glare of sunlight. Justice was a good fifty feet ahead, and Hardistein broke briefly into a trot.

Justice walked straight across parade to where the French horse trader, squatting on his heels before his string, sat watching.

"Didn't think you'd be back," the trader said, rising. "Now, if you're looking for a good piece of horseflesh, eye this chestnut."

Ruff did eye it. It was somewhat gaunted from time spent on the trail without oats and currying, but it was a blooded animal, leggy, deep-chested, wearing a Minnesota brand. He lifted the right hind hoof and stared at it, then slowly lowered the leg.

"No ringhoof on this animal." The trader patted the animal's glossy haunch. "No splits. Look at these teeth, man."

"How long you had him?" Ruff asked.

"Since yesterday." The Frenchman had taken off his hat to scratch his head. Now he put it back on. Slow understanding lit up his dark eyes. "I get it now. It ain't the horse, it's the man you're looking for?"

"That's right," Ruff said. "Do you recall him?"

The Frenchman stroked the chestnut's muzzle. "I recall him. But my business ain't information, mister. It's horses."

Ruff recognized a cue when he heard one. He slipped a gold eagle from his pocket and slapped it into the Frenchman's palm. The horse trader beamed.

"What did he look like?"

"Look like?" The trader shrugged. "Big, burly. Stunk like a goat. Wore a red shirt. Had him a big black mustache and a little thimble nose . . ."

"Tug Slaussen!" Mack Pierce said.

Ruff had forgotten about the soldiers. Now he turned his head slowly toward Pierce and Hardistein.

"It is, isn't it?"

"Damm it. Damm it all!" Mack Pierce said slowly. Slaussen had tried to kill Ruff before. It had happened before the Spirit Woman War. Slaussen and a trooper named Frank Howler had set upon a party of Crow Indians—an old man and three women. One of the women had been raped. The woman was Ruff's sister-in-law. Frank Howler had gotten his, and Tug Slaussen had tried to kill Ruff before the scout could even the score. He had

21

made his try, failed, and gotten away. About that time the Spirit Woman business had flared up, intervening. Slaussen, knowing that Ruff Justice was not a man to forget, had apparently tracked them southward and tried again. This time he had killed Louise.

This time there would be nothing to intervene, nothing to stand between Ruff Justice and the object of his vengeance. Mack Pierce stood to one side, reading the cold determination in Ruff's eyes. He was happy he had not been born with the name Tug Slaussen.

"Funny no one saw him," Hardistein remarked. The man had once been a soldier at Lincoln.

"Hell, it's been a while, Ray," Pierce pointed out. "We've got maybe ten percent of the people we had two years ago when Slaussen mustered out."

"Tell me about it," Ruff said to the Frenchman.

"That's about it," the horse trader answered with a shrug. "A man came in. He had him this nice chestnut, but it was worn down. I traded him a bay, not quite as fine, but fat and woolly. He gave me twenty dollars and rode out with the other three."

"The other three?"

"Yeah. Sure. There were three men waiting here for him. After we dickered they changed saddles and rode out."

"Did you know any of them?"

"Never laid eyes on any of 'em. A hard-lookin' bunch, though. Wait—I heard some conversation. One of them asked if he had taken care of his business. Thimble-nose said well, he thought he had. Then the other one—big man with a flaming red beard, Scotsman I'd guess—said, well, then they had better get along and take care of some business of their own. Off they rode. I didn't pay no more attention to it. This half-breed Cheyenne came in with a string of nubbed-down mustang ponies. I told him . . ."

Ruff Justice was already walking away. "Hey," the Frenchman shouted, "what about this blue roan?"

Justice didn't even look back. Mack Pierce and Ray Hardistein had followed him to his horse. Now, as Justice stepped into the stirrups, Ray said: "Keep your head low, Ruff."

"I mean to, Ray. Tell your major that I've gone."

"Sure. He don't mean nothin', Ruff. He's just a man trying to ride out his career."

"I know it. Tell MacEnroe I stopped by."

"I'll do that. The colonel will be sorry he missed you."

"I'll wager," Ruff said dryly.

"He will. The order? Christ, Ruff, he kind of had to do that, didn't he? After last time, I mean. But he always was fond of you, Ruff. Hell, he knows that you've saved his bacon more'n once. It's just . . . you're too much the lone wolf for the army service, Ruff, and you know it."

"I guess I do," Ruff admitted. "Take care, Ray. Mack." He nodded to the two NCOs and then, clicking his tongue at the gray, he was gone, riding through the crowded parade ground toward the gate. They stood watching him a moment longer before Mack Pierce muttered, "Look out, Tug Slaussen, the man's on your trail," and together the two sergeants walked back toward the headquarters building.

3

THE CLOUDS HAD been building far to the north, and in the brief span of time it took Ruff Justice to ride to Bismarck, they had crept in, roofing over half the sky. Rain looked like a possibility tonight.

He knew what he was looking for now, and who. The trip to Fort Lincoln had been more than worthwhile.

Tug Slaussen. A man Ruff only dimly remembered, but whom he knew well. A murderous bastard, one who preyed on young women. He had two marks against him now, and either was enough to justify his death.

He was riding a bay, a fresh horse, "fat and woolly." He carried a .56 Spencer like Ruff's own carbine. He was riding with three other men, one with a flame-red beard, possibly a Scotsman.

Bismarck was growing, crowds milled in the streets, but even here such a group of men would be recognizable. As Ruff entered the east side of town his eyes flickered from side to side, searching the shadows, the hitch rails, the faces of the men in the street.

Had they come here? It seemed likely, but he couldn't be sure. He had found the tracks of four men traveling together and then lost them. The road from Bismarck to Fort Lincoln was heavily traveled, and the tracks had lost themselves among the hundreds of others. Ruff knew the four tracks could have belonged to anyone, but he had seen no horses leaving the road, riding off into the distance. There weren't many men—not in a party of four—willing to ride into the Sioux homeland just now.

It had to be Bismarck.

Slaussen would be in a hurry to get away from here, but there was a job to do: business to be taken care of, according to the Frenchman.

What kind of business? What kind did men like Slaussen engage in? Robbery, murder, extortion, rape, arson, blackmail . . . some of those possibilities could be weeded out. Robbery stood out as the prime possibility.

Ruff rode slowly past the false-fronted green building with iron bars on the front windows. The Bank of Bismarck. Likely? Ruff didn't know, but it was a distinct possibility. Hit a bank and ride out onto the plains—it would be pure hell trying to raise a posse these days.

He passed a mercantile store which sat on the corner of Main and Front streets. There eight covered wagons were drawn up, loading supplies: flour, sugar, salt, gunpowder, nails, dried fruit. These people were not gold seekers, but sodbusters. Headed where?

Didn't they know about Red Cloud, and about Ta-Shaka, who was reputed to be even worse, a butcher and madman? Ruff saw women and kids sitting on the tailgates of the Conestogas, and he shook his head. Men hungry for land, desperate for it. So desperate that they would challenge the Sioux and Cheyenne. So desperate that they would risk their families' lives.

The hitch rails were crowded. The saloons, old and new, even one still under construction, were doing a boom business. Ruff swung down at the first he came to, a place called the Roughshod.

If you were looking for a man in Bismarck, it seemed, you looked in the saloons. Ruff was looking for a man. He looped his gray's reins over the hitchrail, stepped under, and went up onto the sagging plankwalk.

He eased into the Roughshod, meeting a wall of noise. Every table in this prairie hideout had a card game going. A lopsided roulette wheel spun to a stop to the accompaniment of groans and curses of disappointment. There was the constant clatter of glass against glass. The men were three deep at the rough bar which ran along the far wall. Somewhere a banshee voice rose above the din; it was a time before Ruff realized some faded, buxom rose was standing on a box trying to sing to these sinners.

Ruff eased forward. There were a hundred men in the Roughshod, and perhaps one of them had come there to die.

He made a slow circuit of the saloon, his eyes sharp and piercing, his movements slow. He was jostled by elbows and hips, but he paid no attention to any of it. A short cowboy lay asleep or dead in the corner. No one paid him any mind. Likely he wouldn't be discovered until they swept up.

Nothing.

Ruff circled the room again, and quartering it, he searched it section by section for the third time. No Tug Slaussen.

Ruff hadn't seen the man in a good long time, but he had a fair recall and he could remember the sullen, heavy-featured face of Slaussen. His jowls were heavy, his lips thick and rubbery. His eyebrows were dark thick fringes pasted to an overhanging shelf of brow. Planted incongruously in the dead center of that crude face was a tiny, delicate nose.

Ruff edged over to the end of the bar. He nudged the last man there, an old-timer in galluses and mule-ear boots.

"I'm looking for someone." Ruff described Slaussen, and the old miner looked at him dully through bleary eyes.

"Don't sound familiar. But then I've only been in town three days. I was planning on stickin' it out up there. Had me a dugout in the side of the hill. Nights, I'd drag brush over the opening. Wasn't much, but it was warm enough, and I'd found some color down along . . . well, never mind," he said shrewdly. He took a drink of his green beer and made a wry face. "That lasted up until a week back. I come out of that hole one morning like a prairie dog, feeling bushy. And I tell you I got back in quick!"

"Sioux?"

"I should say. There must have been a thousand of 'em. God, there they sat along the river, watering their ponies. They stayed there a day and a night, and I lay there, my finger on the trigger of my Henry. Not that it would have done me any good." He took another swallow of beer.

"Nobody stirring much out there then?"

"Nobody white! I seen a whole town—such they called it—pick up and leave. It was called Grizzly, population four hundred and four. Not a man left there. Sioux have likely burned it down."

Ruff left the Roughshod and went to the next saloon in the row, searching it as before. There was no sign of Tug Slaussen, although he nearly got caught up in a brawl.

The pattern was repeated at the Bucket of Blood. By the time Ruff came out of there the sun was already beginning to droop toward the western horizon. The purple shadows were creeping out from the base of the building, and he realized he was hungry.

He also realized he was being watched.

There was no doubt about it and no mistaking the man. He carried a shotgun, wore a leather jacket which fell to his knees, and had a patch over one eye. He was hawk-faced, weather-lined, and tough as nails. Tom Dukes, marshal of Bismarck.

He was leaning against a porch upright, watching Ruff narrowly. Ruff ignored him, crossing the street toward the small white building which housed the restaurant calling itself Cousin Anne's.

It was surprisingly empty. It was still early, maybe, or perhaps the men in town didn't see the point in wasting money on food when there was liquor to be had.

Justice took a table in the corner and ordered ham, eggs, and potatoes.

"That 'eggs,'" the weary waitress told him, "is only good when we got eggs."

27

"You don't have eggs?"

"Uh . . . no."

"Ham and potatoes then," he said, offering her a smile, which she didn't seem to care for. As he waited he watched the people around him, those who came and went. Logic said Slaussen would be in Bismarck, but that meant nothing. The problem was that if he wasn't here, the time Ruff spent searching the town was time Slaussen could use to put distance between them. He would know Ruff was behind him. He would know what would happen when he was caught.

He had two choices—to run or to fight. Knowing Slaussen, his idea of fighting Ruff would be to back-shoot him as he walked past a dark alley.

The waitress had returned, slapped down the steaming platter, and angled away toward another table. Ruff's eyes followed her for a moment and then narrowed.

Beautiful? The dark-haired woman who sat at the table was more than that. She was enough to raise a man's blood pressure with a casual glance. A lingering examination of those full, high breasts, broad, sensual mouth, and mocking dark eyes was enough to put one out of commission. She was the kind that addled the brain, made a fool out of you and made you like it.

Ruff had grief for protection, but it wasn't quite enough. When she lifted her eyes and met his gaze he felt a slow steady pulsing begin to throb through his veins.

She said something to the silver-haired man in a dark suit who sat beside her, and he looked toward Ruff. Then the second man's head came up.

His eyes were possessive, jealous, and they flared up as he saw Justice. He was broad-shouldered, dressed in a twill suit which pinched his massive arms. He had washed-out blond hair cut short and a thin mustache.

His gaze was challenging, but Ruff was in no mood for that kind of childish confrontation. He turned his eyes down and began sawing at his slab of ham, finding it tender, deeply smoked, and tasty.

He was nearly finished with his meal, swallowing the

last of his potatoes, which were, unsurprisingly, greasy, when the shadow crossed his table.

He looked up to see the silver-haired man, the woman, and the man with the jealous eyes. It was the older man who spoke.

"Mr. Justice?"

"That's right."

"I told you," the woman said in a soft voice. The blond man looked distinctly unimpressed.

"May we sit down?"

Ruff shrugged, and they did so, the big man drawing a chair from a nearby table to reverse. He leaned across the back of it, massive forearms folded, glaring at Justice. The woman was also watching him, but there was no animosity in her dark eyes. The older man was speaking again.

"This is a stroke of good fortune. Someone told us that Ruffin T. Justice was in town and that he was no longer in the army service."

"True. However . . ."

"Allow me to introduce myself. I am Caleb Waters. My daughter, Abigail, and her husband, Brent Shaughnessy." Ruff nodded, Abigail smiled brilliantly, Shaughnessy glowered.

Waters continued, "You have a wide and glowing reputation, Mr. Justice." Ruff had to smile—"glowing" was not the adjective they would have used at Fort Lincoln.

"Glowing?"

"That is," Waters said, leaning intently forward, "you know the territory, you know the Indians."

"Some."

"I understand you've lived with them."

"Some. The Crow," Ruff replied. "That doesn't mean I'm in the bosom of the entire Indian race." He was starting to get an uncomfortable idea of where this was leading. Waters confirmed the suspicion.

"I understand. However," Waters said, smiling confidently, "your talents and knowledge of the area and its inhabitants are said to be without peer."

That was enough to cause Shaughnessy's glower to deepen again. Abigail Shaughnessy was smiling deeply, in that languorous, soft way which could only be interpreted as an invitation. Ruff had the idea that he wasn't the first man to have that smile cast his way.

"We have therefore decided to approach you," Waters was saying.

"Yes?"

"It is essential that I get through to the Black Hills. To the town of Grizzly." Waters leaned even nearer, his eyes anxious. "You see, I have purchased a sutler's post. The army is determined to establish an outpost at Grizzly within the next year, and if I am not settled there prior to their arrival I will lose my contract—and I may add that bids for sutler's posts are quite high at the present time."

That was true—many a man had gotten rich gouging the troopers. The sutler's stores were a necessary contingent to an army post. They provided a service which was much needed and much desired by the men, who had little else and were glad to spend a portion of their pay for tobacco, tinned food, beer, paper, and ink—a hundred articles. The prices were usually high, and the sutler had a stranglehold on the men. By army regulation no man could muster out unless he had settled any debts with the sutler.

"I appreciate your problem," Ruff said finally. "But I'm not your man."

"You are otherwise occupied?"

"I am. Even if I wasn't, I wouldn't ride those hills right now for any amount of money. When a cavalry company is not safe, no wagon train has a prayer. Do you know what the situation is in Grizzly just now?" Ruff asked.

"Why . . ." Waters blinked in puzzlement. "I understand it is prospering, that there are more than four hundred people living there."

"You've been talking to the wrong folks. Grizzly's practically a ghost town now according to what I hear."

"But . . ."

"Listen, Mr. Waters, I understand your situation, but

no one—no one sane—is going to guide you through to the Black Hills just now. The thing to do is hole up here in Bismarck and wait until the army is ready to actually build that outpost."

"But I have only a year!" Waters said, practically shouting. "My contract will expire if I haven't established a sutler's store by that time."

The man had taken a gamble and had lost. He had bid to establish a store for an as yet nonexistent outpost. How much had it cost him? Was it one of those desperate gambles a man takes, risking all? Ruff had the idea it might have been.

"I'm sorry, Mr. Waters. I'm engaged in some personal business just now. If I were free to guide you through to Grizzly, I wouldn't. It's pure hell out there right now. Count yourself lucky if you lose only money. If you wander out on the plains right now, you'll lose a hell of a lot more than that."

"Goddam coward," Brent Shaughnessy muttered just loud enough to be audible. Ruff's cold eyes flickered to the face of Shaughnessy. For an instant . . . no, it wasn't worth it. Let the fool think whatever he liked.

"Mr. Shaughnessy, if you care for your wife, you'll not allow her to travel out there just now. I assure you the reports that are sifting in are not exaggerations. Any white on the plains is risking his life. A woman risks most. Pain, degradation, and then slow death."

Abigail shuddered. Shaughnessy's lips compressed and he shook his head. "We've got plenty of guns with us. I reckon I can take care of my wife."

Caleb Waters rose and said stiffly, "Thank you for sparing us some of your obviously valuable time, Mr. Justice."

With that they were all gone. Abigail Shaughnessy rose, the amusement in her eyes returning as she said a short goodbye to Ruff. Watching her leave, holding her husband's arm lightly, Justice was happy that he was not responsible for keeping that woman out of trouble. She was born to it. Men had no chance at all with a woman

31

like that; women had very little. She was steeped in sex. Her eyes were a challenge, her body a magnet. She would get a man killed one day; Ruff was only glad it would not be him.

Ruff gave them ten minutes, then, rising, he paid for his meal and left the restaurant, planting his wide black hat on his head. Outside it was dark and cool. Smoke rolled out of the saloons to cloud the streets of Bismarck, and the hooting, the shouting, the drunken laughter assailed the ears.

Ruff sighed. It was enough to make a man go out onto the plains, away from the racket, the brawling, the shrieking, the tinny, repetitious music . . . almost enough.

But his business was here right now. He hadn't forgotten the thug known as Tug Slaussen, the bright-eyed, yellow-haired woman with the gaping hole in her lithe young body. He never would.

Burying Tug Slaussen wouldn't erase the haunting demons; it was only a part of it—a retribution due. Ruff tugged his hat down and crossed the street, watching a dead-drunk cowboy, his boot caught in the stirrup, being dragged past down Bismarck's main street.

The Golden Eagle was next on his list, and he entered through batwing doors to stand in the smoky shadows, watching the miners at play. The interior was identical to those of the other saloons he had visited. Oblong, filthy, smoke-filled, a long puncheon bar. The men might have been the same, the tired girls, the big-shouldered bartender. What a place to waste your life away, he thought.

He moved among them, smelling the sourness of them, seeing their too-bright eyes, finding no hint of common feeling in his own heart for these drunken brawlers. If you looked hard enough you could see the despair.

"Find him yet?"

Ruff turned at the sound of the voice, his hand going lazily toward the butt of his holstered Colt. He didn't need the gun. The speaker wore a dark-brown suit and a brown derby hat. He held a thin cigar negligently in his hand. The other hand was at his stomach, which was flat, crossed by a gold watch chain. One thumb was hooked in a vest pocket.

He spoke with an English accent. He was pure Indian.

"Arikara, aren't you?"

"What's that? Oh, I see, yes, yes, Arikara. Name's Reginald Darby-Smythe," he said, sticking out a dark hand. "Borrowed name, don't you know."

They shook hands. "How did you know I was looking for someone?"

"Oh, that. Ha ha. Well, I haven't lost all of my instincts, you know. I jolly well know when a man is on the hunt. Besides, I heard you asking at the Roughshod—that's my regular pub, you see."

The man was amusing, but Ruff wasn't in the mood to be amused. "I've got to be going," he said tersely.

"Quite. Yes, I understand, mustn't let the quarry escape. But hold on—perhaps I can be of some assistance."

"How?"

"Well, let's discuss it, shall we? Over a glass of bitters. Or whatever barbarian concoction we can find. Gin and tonic, perhaps?"

"I don't drink."

"No? Extraordinary," Reginald Darby-Smythe, the full-blooded Arikara Indian, said, drawling the word out in the best upper-class British manner. "Let's do have a seat, Mr. . . . Justice, did they say?" Ruff nodded. "I do believe the name strikes a chime. Ha ha. Here, here's a table. Hold fast, I'll obtain refreshments."

Ruff sat, watching the Indian move through the crowd to emerge again in minutes, two glasses in his hands. "Here we are, good fellow. Tea—if you drink it. Not exactly the camel's ace here, but one pays the price for a frontier existence. For myself I'll stick to the local favorite—red-eye whiskey. Delightful appellation, what?"

"Delightful." Ruff sipped the tea, found it bordering on acceptable, and removed his hat, placing it on the table top. The Indian was drinking his whiskey, cigar still clenched firmly in his hand. Beyond the window at their elbow Ruff could see two men stagger past, singing an off-key song about cattle and a dead wrangler. There was a third man in that alley, suffering loudly and wretchedly from the result of too much of that local favorite with the delightful appellation.

"Would you prefer another table?" Reginald asked, although every other table Ruff could see was already occupied.

"This one is quite all right." He looked with curiosity at the man across the table from him, a man immaculate in his grooming, one who spoke better English than Ruff himself yet had been born on the plains, not far from where they now sat, for the Arikara were the native local tribe—or had been until the Sioux had run most of them off. Their range was a narrow strip of land along the upper Missouri which had orginally extended from just above Fort Lincoln down to the vicinity of the juncture of the Cheyenne River and the Oahe Lake.

The Ariks hadn't been a fierce people—not that they were cowardly; they weren't, they were among the best warriors Ruff had ever come across—and they hadn't the numbers to hold back the larger tribes like the Sioux and Cheyenne. They had been pushed around quite a bit by everyone until there were only a very few left in the area.

"What exactly is it you think you can do for me, Reginald?" Ruff asked.

The Arik grinned. "Call me, Reggie, old boy. All my pals do. Well, you see, it's been a trifle boring around town lately. Ennui has reared its ugly head. I thought I might offer to assist you in your hunt. I know this town, pal. Almost as well as I know the country around it. Raised here from a suckling whelp, you know. Ha ha."

"I appreciate the offer, but I don't really want any help with this, Reggie. Unless you've seen my man."

"Who?"

"Tug Slaussen. Used to be a trooper at Lincoln, but not for several years."

"No." Reggie shook his head. "The name doesn't chime. I'm only recently back in the colonies, you see.

If he hasn't been among us in the last six months, then I'm afraid you are correct. I can be of no help. Ah, well . . ." He sighed and flung an arm over the back of his chair. "Doomed to perpetual boredom. Even a town so droll as this can become stale."

"I imagine." Ruff made to shake himself free of this too-British Indian. Amusing as Reginald Darby-Smythe was, Ruff had no time for idle conversation. "I'll be on my way now—"

At that moment Ruff saw the Indian coil and spring. He hurled himself across the table, and before Ruff could react the Arik had slammed him to the floor of the saloon. Before they had hit the floor the shots echoed loudly through the room, scattering customers.

There were a dozen shots at least, smashing out the alley window which had been at Ruff's back, sending jagged shards of glass flying across the room. The deadly echoes rolled through the room; the black powder smoke hung heavy.

Ruff was still pinned to the floor, broken glass all around him, the Arik on top of him. Finally Reggie got to his feet.

"I say!" he breathed, producing a handkerchief to wipe his dark forehead. "Bit of a stir, what?"

Justice didn't answer. He kicked out the remainder of the jagged window panes and dove through into the dark alleyway. Two men were racing toward the end of the alley, but before Ruff could bring his Colt level, they were gone. He didn't bother giving chase; they had too much lead and they knew the town.

But he smiled. He stood unmoving in the middle of that alley, the scent of powder smoke still in his nostrils, and he smiled.

The man was here, in Bismarck, and they would meet again.

4

REGGIE WAS STILL standing, waiting, when Ruff came in the back door to the saloon and crossed the glass-strewn room. There was a second man there, and his expression was somewhat darker.

Tom Dukes couldn't wait for Ruff to reach him. He took four long strides to halt before the plainsman. "What the hell is this?" the marshal demanded. His single eye glittered with some turbulent emotion.

"Men tried to shoot me through the window. Reggie here knocked me aside," Ruff said simply.

"He did, did he? And just what in hell is an Indian doing hanging around where they sell liquor?" Dukes demanded. Reggie looked deeply stung by that question. "Never mind that for now. Who shot at you, and why? And just who in hell are you, mister?"

"It's a story of some length," Ruff replied.

"All right. We'll walk on over to my office and you can string it out for me. You know, mister, I've got enough trouble in this goddam town without strangers bringing their private battles here, and that's what this shapes up to be. Am I wrong?"

"You're not wrong."

"No, I didn't think so." Dukes whirled around. "What in hell are all you people looking at? Spread out, give us some room. The party's over!"

He waved his shotgun as he spoke, and it cleared them out quickly. Ruff had to grin. Dukes had this town under his thumb, and that was exactly what he had been hired to do. Dukes was a town-tamer from way back. Deadwood, Turkey Gulch, Beaver Creek—he had turned them all into pink-tea parties. He regularly worked himself out of a job, this man. He had a strong reputation, and almost unique among western marshals, he had the distinction of having never shot a man in the back or from ambush.

Common practice, that—a local lawman sitting on a rooftop or alley, gunning down the badman before the badman had a chance to kill him. Most of the best ones had engaged in this kind of peace-keeping, figuring— justly—that the town they had been hired to protect was better off with a dead outlaw and a live marshal.

It was not Tom Dukes's way, however, or at least that was his reputation, and if it made some folks admire his courage, it made others wonder how long the damned fool would survive.

The marshal's office was made of cast-off lumber and bricks. He had a single cell, the door of solid oak with a dozen airholes bored through it. Someone seemed to be sleeping one off behind it; the buzzsaw snoring floated through the ramshackle office.

"Hell of a nice place, isn't it?" Dukes asked with a wry smile. His tough exterior had softened the moment Ruff entered the office. His street face was put aside and Ruff saw only a lean, weatherbeaten, weary man who wore a badge pinned to a once-white shirt beneath that leather coat.

Dukes opened a desk drawer, offered whiskey, and shrugged when Ruff shook his head. He sat in his chair and in the time-honored way of the peace officer, tilted back and propped his black boots on the desk.

"Now just what in hell have we got?" Dukes asked.

"My name's Ruff Justice," Ruff began. Then he ran through it from beginning to end, stumbling a bit over the murder. Still she could come back strongly, vividly, to his mind. Her golden hair shining in the morning sunlight, spread out across the green spring grass . . .

"You're sure it was Slaussen?" Dukes asked at the end.

"Positive. I trailed him to Lincoln, talked to the man who bought his horse."

"And he's here now?"

"It does seem so," Ruff answered dryly.

"What's Lord Reggie got to do with this?"

"Nothing. We were just talking. He saved my life, I guess. He was trying to invite himself into the fight, and I refused."

"Going to do it all yourself, are you?" the marshal asked.

"I planned on it." Ruff's eyes were cold.

"Yeah. I can understand that. But we've got a problem, Mr. Justice."

"Oh?" Ruff lifted an eyebrow.

Dukes drummed his fingers on the desk top, reached down and refilled his glass, and went on, "You kill a man in my town, you'll hang for it, partner."

"Without a trial?"

"Oh, there'll be a trial. Thing is the folks around here favor them short and sweet. They also like there to be a . . . what should I say . . . entertaining conclusion to their trials."

"It's a hangtown."

"More or less. It livens things up."

"There's more to it," Ruff said after studying Dukes for a time.

"Is there?" Dukes peered at him from out of the shadows.

"I think so. You didn't bring me in here just to threaten me. You're not telling me something."

"All right." Dukes stood and leaned against the wall, which was plastered with curled wanted posters and notices. "Let's say I was trying to get the feel of you, Justice. I wanted to see what kind of man you are."

"And?" Ruff asked with a thin smile.

"You'll do," Dukes answered flatly. He came forward

to the desk again, his face thoughtful. The buzzsaw snoring continued in the cell beyond. "This is what I want to know—is Slaussen riding with another man?"

"Three others."

"What do they look like?"

"No idea, really. I was given a description," Ruff answered, crossing his legs. "On one of them, that is. Big man with a flame-red beard."

Dukes cursed softly. "MacAdoo."

"Who?"

"Amos MacAdoo. He's big trouble, believe me. We've run into each other before." Dukes planted his butt on the corner of his desk. "Have you any idea what they're up to, Justice?"

"None at all. It didn't concern me, actually. I know that Tug Slaussen had met up with three men, one of them possibly this MacAdoo—if the description fits." Dukes nodded. "Besides that, all I heard was that they had some 'business' to take care of."

"You can bet they do." Dukes fished around in his top desk drawer and produced a half cigar, which he proceeded to light, scratching the match across the desk top. "The MacAdoo gang has been prowling the border area for the last year or so. It's the banks that interest them mostly, and they've had a fair amount of luck. Now and then they'll hit a settlers' train or an outfitter—general stores and such, they sometimes have a fair amount of cash—but mostly it's the banks."

Dukes rose and went on. "The banks in this part of the country, as you know, Justice, are little more than crackerboxes. Built the same as everything else out of used lumber . . . some are only tents with a strongbox. MacAdoo finds them pretty easy prey. He hits them and then rides into Indian territory. He must have a hole out there somewhere, but no one's been able to locate it. Haven't tried that hard—you'd be surprised how shy people are about joining a posse heading into Sioux territory."

"Smart," Ruff acknowledged, "but dangerous. Is MacAdoo that brave or is he plain mad?"

Tom Dukes's face pulled itself into a harsh mask. "A little of both, I'm afraid. He's a rough one, Justice. Big and dirty and vicious. He'd as soon kill a woman as an armed man. He's been known to take scalps. He's pure mean and pure trouble."

"Well?" Ruff looked steadily at Dukes. The marshal took a deep, noisy breath through his nostrils. He didn't answer, so Ruff asked plainly: "Why are you telling me any of this, Dukes?"

"Because you're after Slaussen. You want him bad. So do I. Slaussen, Granger, and Crowder. Not to mention Amos MacAdoo."

"And?"

"I want you to put a badge on."

Ruff laughed out loud. He slowly shook his head. "Can't do it, Dukes. When I find Slaussen it won't be an arrest. It'll be plain murder."

"What makes you think I object to that?" Dukes asked, his eyes nearly as cold as those of Ruff Justice. "It's not murder with this kind. We can arrest them and bring them in, but they'll hang anyway. Deservedly. They're not men, Justice, not this breed. They're vermin. They deserve to be stomped flat, crushed."

Justice was quiet for a minute, reading the vehemence in Dukes's voice. "What'd he do to you, Tom? What did Amos MacAdoo do to hurt you?"

"It was my brother, Justice," Tom said. "They snatched the kid. He was the one going to stay away from guns, stay away from violence—he hated it. Hated me, likely. He got him a job in a bank. Just a nice young kid trying to save up enough money to get hitched on.

"They took him hostage, and it was a week before I found him." Dukes's single eye glittered. It reminded Ruff then of the jeweled eye of a rattlesnake on the prod. "He was done up worse than any Indian would have done. They scalped him, Justice, cut his tongue out . . . his fingers were . . . the bastard!" Dukes hissed. Ruff let him regain himself.

"I won't put on a badge. It implies a certain duty," Justice said again. "When I find Slaussen, he's my meat, totally."

"All right," Dukes argued. "Think of this—a badge gives you immunity of a sort. You'll kill him if you find him, sure. But suppose they want to hang you for that? Suppose you have to die to wipe that scum off the earth? It's no good, Justice."

Ruff, despite himself, felt uncomfortable. He felt like some vigilante meeting in a deserted barn. Tom Dukes's hatred was obviously every bit as deep as his own. The man continued to puff on his cigar even though it had long ago gone dead.

"What's this 'business' they've got to do?" Ruff asked.

Dukes shrugged. "Tell me. I figure it must be the bank, but I don't know. Whatever it is they won't wait long, will they? They know you're in town hunting Slaussen. And by now they know we've talked." Dukes words were almost pleading. "Help me, Justice."

Ruff was long in responding. "If they take off into the Sioux territory, the badge isn't worth a dime."

"No. But no judge would hang a lawman pursuing the MacAdoo gang. Hell, there's no law at all out there." He looked past his narrow, barred window toward the dark plains.

"Pin it on," Ruff said finally. He still didn't like the idea, didn't like working for another man, didn't like the weight of a badge, but in the end Dukes's arguments had swayed him.

It wasn't pinned on, that badge. Dukes simply flipped him a town marshal's star and Ruff shoved it into his shirt pocket.

Dukes rose, taking another shotgun from his gunrack. Without turning his head he told Ruff: "I'm damned glad you took that, Justice. Otherwise, you know, I would have locked you up. I can't have civilians getting in the way. Let's eyeball the bank."

He tossed Ruff the shotgun and they went out. Walking toward the bank, they kept to the alleys and the shadows. The bank itself, as Dukes had told him, was built no more

41

strongly than a stable. There were bars in the windows, but Ruff had the idea a horse could pull them out easily enough.

Looking at the dilapidated building, Ruff wondered how much money could be in there. But then the refugees from the Black Hills gold digs had placed part of their pokes in there. Too, the people like the Waters party—and thinking of them brought back a surging memory of Abigail—would have put their traveling money, their provision money, in the bank temporarily. No sense being knocked over the head when there was a bank in Bismarck.

Dukes held out a hand, and Ruff halted. They were standing at the end of the narrow, horse-smelling alley directly across the street from the bank. Beyond the bank Ruff could see the big oaks swaying gently in the breeze, see the starlit river rolling southward, dark and inexorable.

Dukes pointed a finger. "Two guards. One outside, one in."

Squinting, Ruff could see the lazy, lean man sitting in a chair in front of the bank, rifle across his lap. He wouldn't be much of a deterrent to a dedicated thief.

There was a faint glow at a side window, the second guard, probably dozing or at least inattentive.

"I told the dumb bastards . . ." Dukes whispered. His voice broke off abruptly as a gliding shadow broke free of the surrounding darkness and came up to meet them.

Ruff could see the vague outline of a derby hat and little else, but he knew who it was.

"What in hell are you doing here, Reggie?" Dukes demanded in a hiss.

"Had the feeling something was up when I saw you two sneaking around with those scatterguns."

"Why don't you scoot on off now?"

"Why, marshal, I thought you gentlemen would be pleased at my arrival. I saw them, you know."

Dukes spun on the Indian. "Saw who?"

"MacAdoo, that savage," Reggie replied as if slightly bored by it. "Who else?"

"Where?"

"They're gone now, Marshal. Please do let go of my coat. They were holding a soirée behind the Western Trails Stable just as I was preparing to lie down for the evening."

"He sleeps in the stable," Dukes said by way of explanation.

"Only temporary lodgings," Reggie replied. "I haven't yet located a suitable abode."

"Get on with it," Dukes said irritably.

"It's tonight they mean to accomplish their banditry, marshal. I did notice," he added, "that their ranks have swollen. MacAdoo has six in his band now."

"All right," Dukes said, "we can still handle it. Spread out a little. Ruff, why don't you try circling into the oaks behind the bank? Reggie, since you're here, hold down the fort here. I'll ease up beside the saddlery where I'll have a good line of fire all up the street. Move it and stay low. They'll have no lack of ammunition and they'll be willing to burn it up."

Ruff was on his way even before Dukes finished. He emerged from the end of the silent alley and crossed the open space beyond, working through the sage and greasewood brush until he reached the river.

Then, the sounds of croaking frogs echoing in his ears, he moved northward and swung around until he was able to creep up through the mammoth wind-ruffled oaks toward the rear of the dark bank. He eased his way to the very edge of the grove, and there, crouched in the shadows, he was able to see the rear of the bank. He could not see Reggie or Tom Dukes and had not expected to.

The hours passed slowly. Once a drunk on a sway-backed mule came hooting into town, and Ruff felt the nerve in his index finger twitch. That finger was curved around the cool trigger of the ten-gauge express gun, and he was glad it hadn't twitched a hair more.

He was wondering about the wisdom of the shotgun

now; he was fifty yards from the bank and would have preferred his Spencer carbine.

A coyote howled once far away, and a town dog yapped back excitedly. From uptown there was a crash and a following curse. The mist was drifting in from off the river now and the stars were hidden behind a twisting haze.

And then he saw them. One man, riding a pale horse, walking it lazily toward the bank. Ruff watched him, his senses alert. The man was too narrowly built to be either Slaussen or MacAdoo. He rode on past, whistling, saying a word Ruff would not make out to the bank guard.

Then he was gone. Ruff thought he heard another horse shuffle its feet behind the hardware store adjacent to the bank, but he could see nothing.

The horse was returning from the river, its rider waving a friendly hand to the guard. It was all Ruff could do to keep from calling out a warning and giving himself away—for he knew what would happen next.

The friendly cowpuncher halted his horse, pointed toward the river, and then drew his gun and fired twice at point-blank range.

The guard screamed and threw his arms out as the roar of the gun, the flaming tongues of red heat, tore the night apart. They were there suddenly, three from the east, three from the west. The bandits rode toward the bank at a dead run.

Ruff heard a gun explode from across the street, saw one of the riders go down in a crumpled heap. He himself fired at a nearby man and then darted toward the bank, wanting to be closer with that scattergun. From the front of the bank the sounds of constant gunfire erupted. They seemed not to have spotted Ruff yet, however.

He hit the back door of the bank and it sprang open. There was a wire grill in front of him, and beyond that he could see the second guard sprawled dead against the floor, see two masked men stuffing money and gold sacks into a burlap bag.

Their heads came around, and as they did Ruff touched off. The scattergun spewed flame and destruction, blowing the bandits back against the wall. Paper money fluttered down, and black smoke rolled through the bank. A face appeared in the window and Ruff fired again, hearing the yowl of pain, the screamed command.

"Get the hell out of here. Grange!"

"Here." This conversation was punctuated by gunfire and then broken off as if sheared by a sharp knife. There was silence. Only the distant drumming of hoofs and the more distant sounds of men shouting.

Ruff exited the back door cautiously, not wanting to be mistaken for a bandit himself. In fact, it seemed a good time for it and he loosely pinned the badge onto his buckskin shirt.

Running in a low crouch around the buildings, he nearly tripped over a lifeless crumpled form. He crouched, assured himself the man—one he had never seen—was dead, and then moved on.

The guard was sprawled against the dirt road, blood staining the earth black. Reggie was walking slowly toward him, shotgun in the crook of his arm as if he had been hunting pheasant. Down the street a crowd of armed men were stampeding toward the bank.

Ruff heard the groan first. He exchanged a glance with Reggie, and the two of them dashed to where he lay.

"Bastards," Tom Dukes managed to mutter.

His face had been torn open by a bullet. His jaw hung slackly. Blood smeared his shirt front. A second bullet had ripped into the lawman's chest. Pink blood frothed from his broken mouth. Heart and lungs, Ruff knew.

"Got careless," Dukes murmured, "I saw the son of a bitch and I wanted him. Wanted him too much, it looks like. He got away?" He looked hopefully at Ruff.

"He got away," Ruff had to tell him.

"Damn him . . . damn the bastard!" Then Dukes began to cough, choking on his own blood. He sagged back in Reggie's arms and seemed to go out. Suddenly his dark eyes flickered open again and he clutched at Ruff's sleeve. "You . . . you got to get MacAdoo for me, Justice. You've got to get him, stomp him into the ground. . . ."

"I will."

"Swear it!" Dukes's hand clamped desperately on Ruff's forearm. Justice was aware of the crowd around them now, of the dully flickering lanterns, of the buzz of conversation.

"I swear it," Justice said, his mouth feeling dry and cottony. Tom Dukes seemed to smile, his crushed jaw working randomly for a moment. Then his hand slid away and he lay there staring at Ruff with unseeing eyes.

Ruff shook his head and stood up. Reggie caught his eye, and Ruff nodded. Reggie lay the marshal back on the cold ground. "Let's have a look at what we got," Ruff said.

Borrowing a lantern, they examined the faces of the man outside and the two dead inside the bank.

"Know them?" Ruff asked.

Reggie shook his head, but one of the townspeople volunteered, "That tough's name is Paul Weeks. He's been hanging around town for a month or so."

"Looks like he'll be hanging around for a while longer," Ruff replied.

Of the two inside, one had had his face altered in such a way that no one could identify him. The second was also a local.

"Joe Savage's boy—Jesus! This will kill old Joe."

Ruff had been going through the faceless man's pockets and finally came up with something—a bill of sale for a roan horse, fifteen and a half hands, made out to Wilson J. Burke.

Ruff showed it to Reggie. "Yes, I think this is Burke. The build is correct."

"I was hoping maybe we had MacAdoo or Slaussen and didn't even know it. As usual it looks like the generals have skated clean away. Bury them," he added to a nearby townsman. The man nodded solemnly, and within minutes they were clearing the dead away.

"Well?" They sat in the marshal's office in what had

been nearly dead silence. Ruff had taken it upon himself to send the drunk on his way.

"Well what?" Justice asked. He had his feet on the marshal's desk, his hat on his boot toe, his fingers interlaced.

"Are you going to do it, dear fellow?"

"Find MacAdoo?" Ruff lifted an eyebrow, lowered it, and nodded. "Yes, I am. I promised the man."

"I am relieved. I know how easy it is to make a deathbed promise. Few are ever fulfilled."

"This one will be."

Reggie had taken his derby off, and his blue-black hair, barbered and plastered to his skull, gleamed in the lanternlight.

"Have you considered this, Justice? Slaussen and MacAdoo may very well have split up after the abortive bank raid. That is, if you follow Slaussen you may well miss MacAdoo and vice versa." Reggie leaned forward, his black eyes inquisitive.

"Yes, I've considered that," Ruff said finally. "But if I find one he'll tell me where the other is . . . assuming I can find any of them. Grange and Crowder were there, after all. How do we know that one of them didn't kill the marshal? I want them all." Ruff's eyes were cold and solemn, a glittering blue in the faint light.

"At first light then?" the Arik asked.

"You're not going, Reggie."

"Oh, yes I am, old man!" Reggie said with a deal of emphasis. "I do not mean to disparage your no doubt considerable abilities, but I should like to point out that I know this area better than any other man alive. I am without parallel as a tracker. Also, you are pursuing a band of man who outnumber you. Besides," he added slyly, "if you don't take me, I shan't give you a description of the other two men. I know Grange and Crowder both, you see."

"There's others in town who do, I expect."

"Ah, but that will take time, Mr. Justice. Let's not toy with one another, I am going. I have been rather restless of late," he added, stretching his arms over his head. "It might stir up the old juices to aid you in your search. Just the thing for the mounting boredom."

Ruff nodded. He had his eyes on the Indian still, watching the casual expression on Reggie's face. "Why, Reggie? Why do you want to go?"

"Because I loved the man, dammit!" he exploded. "Tom Dukes was the only man in this town who treated me like a human being!" He gained control of himself. Smoothing back his hair with a long sigh, he said cheerily, "First light, then. Don't dally, Mr. Justice—there'll be much to do if we hope to catch these foxes, what?"

And then he was gone. Ruff watched the closed office door for a long minute. Then he rose and blew out the lantern. Stretching out on the bunk in Tom Dukes's cell, he tried to get some sleep. He would need all the rest he could get. Reggie was right about one thing—it would take some doing to catch those "foxes."

If MacAdoo followed his usual pattern, he would head for his hole on the plains. The hideout had never yet been discovered, and it was reasonable to assume that Mac-Adoo—and Slaussen—would return to it.

That left Ruff with only a few points to worry about: a pair of mad-dog killers, a thousand square miles of rough country, and about ten thousand roving Sioux warriors. He managed to sleep anyhow.

5

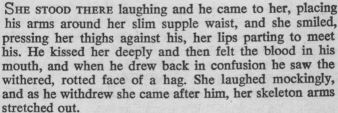

She stood there laughing and he came to her, placing his arms around her slim supple waist, and she smiled, pressing her thighs against his, her lips parting to meet his. He kissed her deeply and then felt the blood in his mouth, and when he drew back in confusion he saw the withered, rotted face of a hag. She laughed mockingly, and as he withdrew she came after him, her skeleton arms stretched out.

They came from the woods then, hundreds of them, and they all carried rifles. They opened fire even as the hag wrapped her arms around Ruff, whispering filth into his ear, and he clawed at his holster, trying to bring his Colt up. He drew his gun, finally shoving the specter away. She sat on the earth, cackling, her clothing and bones crumbling to dust, and the Colt in Ruff's hand melted away, running like hot blood across his hand. . . .

He awoke in a sweat. The dark shadow loomed over him. He started to spring up, felt the hand on his shoulder and heard the voice.

"Easy, old sport. Had a rough night, did you?"

Ruff rubbed his eyes and swung his feet to the side of the bunk without answering. It was very early. No gray showed through the single high window of the marshal's office as of yet.

"You ready?" Ruff asked.

"All ready, old man. Unless you want to stop and breakfast—but I did bring plenty of supplies, food included."

"Then we'll eat on the trail," Ruff said. "I'll get on down and get my horse."

"Already done," Reggie said. "I took the trouble," he said, gesturing at the coffeepot sitting on the small iron stove in the corner. "I do hope you are a coffee man."

"I am this morning." He accepted a tin cup from Reggie, and as he sipped it he studied the Arik, puzzled by the man. By the time they had finished, the gray of false dawn was in the morning skies. Ruff poured the leftover coffee into the woodstove, putting out the smoldering fire.

"It's time," Ruff said, and together they marched out into the predawn grayness. Reggie had changed his clothes. He still wore his brown derby, but his shirt was black, with sleeve garters above the elbows. He wore buckskin pants without fringes and had a high-riding Colt belted on. He had moccasins on his feet and a small orange feather poked into his hatband.

"Rather savage, but one must bow to local conditions," Reggie said, noticing Ruff's appraising eye.

The gray looked rested and ready for some long traveling. Reggie's paint was a walleyed, woolly animal with an evil temper. It tried to bite the Arik's leg as he mounted, and Reggie casually slapped the muzzle away.

"Dreadful," he muttered. "What I'd give for a decent chaser."

They walked the horses down the main street of Bismarck, aware of the scant early-morning activity. One red-eyed saloonkeeper was sweeping the night's collection of garbage out into the street. A kid with a fishing pole, barefoot and happy, dashed out of an alley and ran toward the river. No school today.

Ruff nearly rode past the eight wagons before he realized what was going on. He touched Reggie on the shoulder and reined in.

"Waters?"

Caleb Waters, a case of goods in his hands, turned his strong face toward Ruff and the Indian.

"Good morning, Mr. Justice," he said with a touch of ice in his tone.

"Busy."

"We're heading for Grizzly. We have found a scout willing to undertake the journey."

"A scout? Mr. Waters, you must have found yourself a crazy man. The plains are thick with Indians, and there's no secret about it. You can ask anyone in Bismarck——"

"We've already had your advice," a second voice interrupted. Ruff turned his head to see Brent Shaughnessy, his wife on his arm, glaring at him. "We've had your advice and we don't need it. There are twenty armed men going with us. I assure you we will get through to Grizzly. Besides, our scout says the Sioux are far north of here."

"How in hell does anyone know where they are?" Ruff asked. Shaughnessy ignored him. Abigail Shaughnessy was far from doing that. She stared at Ruff, her eyes inviting, her hips tilted to one side, sheathed in a pair of made-over man's jeans. As a general rule Ruff hated to see women in pants as he did from time to time. Not many could carry it off. Abigail was the exception, and a prime exception. The white pleated blouse did nothing to hide her rather astonishing attributes.

She caught Ruff's appraising eyes on her and smiled more deeply.

It would be a shame to turn that over to the Sioux, he thought before turning his eyes away. The sutler was still staring, arms akimbo, at Justice.

"Mr. Waters——"

"I believe my son-in-law has told you exactly how we feel, Mr. Justice. You refused the job we offered you. I can't see how you can presume to offer us advice, advice based on obviously mistaken information."

"Waters," Justice said, leaning his hands on the pommel of his saddle, "I'm not mistaken. You only want to believe that I am. You'd believe anyone who promised to guide you through to Grizzly.

51

"I'll tell you one last time, and I can only hope that you'll listen. There's war-mad Sioux and Cheyenne on the plains out there, thousands of them. It's as bad as any time in memory in the vicinity of the Black Hills. If you give a damn about your own neck and about your daughter, you won't risk it for the sake of a few dollars."

"All right," Waters said, obviously barely under control. "You've had your say." The vein in his forehead pulsed, his face was a deep crimson. "Now I'll have mine. Get the hell away from me and stay away. I don't believe a damned word you say; I think you're after something. I don't know what, but I think you have your own reasons for keeping me from traveling to Grizzly. And I'm damned if I'll put any credence in anything you have to say, *Mr.* Justice!"

Ruff turned away without saying anything else. The dawning sun was warm on their backs. They had reached the end of the street before Reggie remarked: "White man heap crazy, me think."

"As crazy as we are?" Ruff asked, twisting in the saddle.

"Ah . . ." Reggie chuckled. "That is debatable, isn't it, old man?"

As the sun reddened and cast a bloody glow upon the low eastern clouds the two men moved out onto the prairie. The trappings of civilization fell away abruptly. The scent of sage replaced the smoke and staleness of the town. The air seemed immediately colder, more alive. Away from the trail which led westward toward the Black Hills and Grizzly there was no sign of man to be seen. No bottle, hoofprint, tin can, or litter.

They split up and criss-crossed the western edge of town, their eyes fixed to the ground they traveled over as the sun climbed higher, paling and condensing, growing hotter. They had been at this for an hour when Reggie whistled and Ruff turned his gray horse toward the coulee where the Indian waited, hand lifted in signal.

"Find them?"

"It must be them, old man, but . . . ?" Reggie indicated

the tracks he had located in the soft sand along the edge of the coulee. Ruff got down and squinted first at the tracks and then at the man sitting the paint pony.

"Only three sets of tracks," Ruff said thoughtfully. He looked slowly around, walking his gray up the coulee and down.

"Why?" He looked again at the silent Reggie. "Mac-Adoo, Slaussen, Grange, and Crowder. One of them's not in the bunch." And he had a sinking feeling that it was Slaussen. Slaussen might have been the odd man out, the one who was not a regular member of the gang.

"What do you propose to do?" Reggie asked. He had produced a curving pipe from his vest and was carefully packing the vast bowl with tobacco.

"No choice." Ruff dusted his hands, rose, and stepped into the saddle. "We'd never track a single man in a different direction. We don't know what the tracks look like, where he's heading. These, on the other hand," Ruff said and nodded at the tracks, "have to be the MacAdoo gang. Nobody else is riding westward just now."

One or the other of them had to be in front of them. MacAdoo or Slaussen, and Ruff had vowed to ride down both of them. This might not finish things, but it was a start. Wordlessly he headed out, the long shadow of his horse preceding him across the plains. The Arik, silently smoking his pipe, rode beside him.

"Look there," Reggie said after they had gone a mile or so, and Ruff, turning in the saddle, looked back toward Bismarck. Eight covered wagons with a half-dozen outriders were moving out onto the plains. Caleb Waters and his party.

"The damned fool," Ruff muttered. He started his horse again, thinking briefly of the sultry Abigail. After a mile or so he had forgotten her completely; his thoughts were only on the tracking and the dangerous men who rode ahead.

They stopped at noon at Reggie's insistence, shared a pot of coffee, sliced bacon, and cold biscuits. They ate silently while the unsaddled horses grazed on what sparse gramma grass there was. The sun was high and fierce even in the shade of the bedraggled cottonwood where they ate. The gnats had found them and they swarmed furiously about eyes, ears, mouth, landing in food and drink alike.

They halted for only half an hour, then rose and moved westward again, tugging hats low against the glare of the descending sun.

The tracks were easy to follow now. The plains stretched out endlessly, and the MacAdoo gang rode in a straight line. From the length of the horses' strides they knew that MacAdoo was not moving fast.

Occasionally Ruff glanced northward. The clouds, which had been building constantly, threatening and then withdrawing, still hung on the northern horizon. From time to time distant thunder sounded ominously.

"I hope that holds off for a day or so," Justice said. Just long enough to find them. Long enough to bury them. It was an hour later that they found the Indian sign.

"Six horses," Reggie said. He had gotten down to have a look after Ruff spotted the unshod horse prints. His arm lifted north and west.

"Why?"

Reggie shrugged. "I think maybe these men are scouting the fort, Mr. Justice. Maybe the town was under observation. You will note," Reggie said, rising, "that it's no difficult task to see the roads leading out of Bismarck from this vantage point."

Reggie was right. On this low knoll the view was good across the flats all the way to Bismarck and beyond. Perhaps the Sioux war leader, Ta-Shaka, had posted men here to watch for signs of troop movements. Lincoln was quiet now. What would they have seen to make them ride homeward?

"The Waters wagon train."

Ruff looked at the Arik and slowly nodded. "An easy target. A dozen men, wagons heavily loaded with goods."

"And what do we do, old man?" Reggie asked.

"What can we do?" Ruff's eyes narrowed.

"We owe them a warning."

"They've been warned," he said more harshly than he intended. "And they didn't listen. Besides," he added, "what have we got to tell them? That we saw the sign of a half-dozen Indian ponies. They'd never listen."

"Sioux," Reggie said as they started their horses again. "I despise the bloody Sioux, old man."

Ruff was silent, sensing that Reggie was digging around in his memories. The Arik's mouth formed a bitter line. His black eyes gleamed dully.

"They came when I was a lad," the Indian said. "Before the Americans had approached this area. Took many scalps, they did. My father's and my mother's among them."

Reggie lighted his pipe again, leaning back easily in the saddle. The wind toyed with his blue-black hair.

"What happened to you?"

"Ah." He waved an arm. "Those were difficult times indeed, Mr. Justice. We ran south, what was left of my tribal community. Our homes had been burned, our food stores destroyed, our horses taken.

"Miserable wretches that we were, the gods afflicted us still more. Plague. Some rotten infectious thing. Caused people to break out in boils, to go blind. It was odious, Mr. Justice, in the extreme.

"There were very few of us left by the time we crossed the Big White River. The Sioux again—Teton Lakota this time—struck, and most of our men were killed in a skirmish. During one attack I was hidden by an aunt beneath a pile of brush. I lay there huddled throughout the night, and when I emerged I found only death and destruction. The dead strewn about the field. I was quite alone after that.

"I returned north. I don't know what called me back to the land of my birth, but I made my way along the river, walking at nights, sleeping hidden in thickets during the day. Many times I was nearly discovered by Sioux.

"I lived alone for a good long time after that. Then when Bismarck began to prosper I went into this white town—searching for any sort of human companionship, I suppose."

Ruff listened silently. Reggie was leaving out much. The suffering, the fear of this lost child must have been great. Yet he had survived and wandered into the white man's company. They couldn't have treated him well either.

"One day I met him. Lord Chalmers, that is. He and his lovely daughter, Elena. They found me quite amusing, I suppose. I acted as serving boy to Chalmers, and when he returned to England, I was taken. Oh, they dressed me up in feathers and paint—I suppose I was quite a trophy. They certainly made a fuss over me in London. A novelty."

That too must have been degrading, but Reggie's tone reflected none of it. After all, he was being fed and coddled. He had it better than in any time before.

"I *loved* it, Mr. Justice. Loved Britain. I became convinced that I should have been born there. The quintessential Anglophile!"

"What happened to bring you back?"

"What happened?" Reggie mused. "*Cherchez la femme,* Mr. Justice."

"Woman trouble."

"Exactly. Elena Chalmers had grown into an exquisite beauty. We had been childhood playmates—soon it became more than that."

"Her father didn't care for it."

"Not at all, sport!" Reggie laughed. "I was no longer amusing. Run out of the islands, I was. Damned lucky I wasn't tarred and feathered. Chalmers gave me a ruddy great speech about gratitude and then handed me a ticket to the colonies." Reggie sighed. "And so here I am, home again. A man without a country, without a home. A red Englishman, if you like."

It couldn't have been easy to come back. Was there ever a figure more open to mockery—Reginald Darby-Smythe, the Indian who paraded around acting like some highborn Englishman. The townspeople must have—

"Look out!" Reggie shouted the warning just as the Sioux burst up out of the coulee. The first arrow passed so near to Ruff's head that he could hear the angry buzz as it spun by.

Ruff went low over the withers of the gray, turning it roughly to his right so that he could drop down behind it. He fired beneath the gray's neck as the war cries filled the air.

Reggie was in front of him, firing from horseback, the carbine barking methodically. Ruff saw one wildly painted Sioux throw out his hands and scream. His chest exploded with gore and he bounced from his pony to be ridden over by the men behind him.

Ruff fired twice and saw his target go down in a heap. He had taken the Sioux's war pony in the chest, and the buckskin faltered, misstepped, and then rolled, throwing his rider free.

Ruff reared and fired twice at the Indian, watching him topple and die. Reggie, coming abreast of a Sioux, had flung himself through the air, his derby sailing free. He had hit the man with his shoulder, and the impact took them both to the ground.

Ruff rode toward him, firing his last round at the lone remaining attacker. The .44 took him in the throat and he was dead before he hit the ground, his pony, kicking up its heels, running free across the plains.

Reggie had his man by the hair, and as Ruff dismounted at a run, he saw the Arik's knife flash, saw the dreadful crimson slash appear across the Sioux's throat.

The Sioux convulsed and then lay still. Reggie was on top of him, his knee in his chest, breathing wildly, his eyes wide. He took the scalp then, neatly, savagely, revealing the white skull beneath.

Then, as Ruff watched, the Arik turned, holding high the knife and the enemy scalp. His head was thrown back, his eyes nearly shut. Then he began to chant, to sing, his voice wavering, rising and falling methodically. As he sang his feet moved rhythmically, and the Arik, reverting to some primitive tribal memory, sang his death song, his song of victory.

Slowly Reggie came around. His eyes cleared and his arms lowered. He blinked at Ruff and then at the scalp he still held.

"Sorry, old man," he said sheepishly. "I seem to have forgotten myself. Ugh." He dropped the scalp. "Filthy thing. Primitive custom, what?"

Then as Ruff watched he searched for his derby, dusted it off, and put it on squarely.

"Ready to ride, old boy?"

6

AFTER LOOKING OVER the dead Sioux, they rode westward again. Ruff was worried. There had been five dead Indians left behind. That meant there was one who had gotten away, one who had not remained behind to pick off the easy prey—two white men, one a city dweller. One who would carry the word to Ta-Shaka that a wagon train was traveling west from Bismarck, into the heart of Sioux territory.

They slept lightly that night atop a low knoll, the horses hobbled nearby. After midnight it began to rain. A slow gray mist which seeped into their bones and obscured the plains. It wasn't enough—yet—to wash away the tracks left by the three bandits.

They ate in the predawn darkness and were on the trail at first light. The world was gray, damp, empty. They plodded on, now having to ford freshets at every low point.

"This weather, we'd ride right up on them before we ever saw them," Ruff said accurately.

Reggie didn't answer. He had withdrawn into himself a little since the scalp-dance incident. Ashamed of the reversion, Ruff thought, wondering about the man now called Reginald Darby-Smythe who paraded around in that brown derby hat. Maybe Lord Reggie had found out something about himself during that brief, primitive bloodletting.

The wind began to pick up, slinging the rain against their bodies, stinging cheeks and exposed hands. The clouds had lowered dramatically, seeming to hover just above the earth. The ground was boggy, and Ruff wondered how the wagon train was doing.

He hadn't thought of it before, but just where had they found a scout for the trail to Grizzly? Who would it have been? He shuffled through his mental file of available, competent men and could come up with no one he knew of who was in the area.

That was *their* problem, he thought angrily. He returned his concentration to his own. The tracks of the men were still evident, pressed deeply into the soft deadgrass plains, but their tracking was necessarily slower now. At times the rain, light as it was, gusted in so that Ruff could barely see Reggie on his right hand.

By noon they were moving at a crawl. It was no good, but Ruff couldn't let go. He kept seeing the eyes of Marshal Tom Dukes, remembering the promise.

Yet riding with him was the nagging realization that one of the four—MacAdoo, Grange, Crowder or Slaussen—had gone his own way. Slaussen could be fifty miles in the opposite direction by now. He could have taken the stage to . . . there was no sense thinking about it now. Self-doubt can kill a man, making him ineffective and useless.

"You chose your path, son," he told himself. "Do what has to be done."

Grimly he clamped his teeth together and heeled the gray forward through the slowly closing veil of weather.

By afternoon they were walking, poking around, casting back and forth, searching for the scattered, rain-blurred prints left by the three killers.

Ruff squatted on his heels, watching Reggie, now wearing a rain slicker as was Ruff, shake his head at the edge of the swiftly flowing whitewater stream. The rain had begun falling in buckets. They were up against it now, and both men knew it.

"Well?" Ruff called above the wash of rain.

Reggie shouted back, pointing across the river. "We can't do much, old man. Perhaps we might pick up the trail farther on if the rain ceases tomorrow."

Follow the general direction of the killers. Hope to cut fresh sign once the rain halted. If it did. Ruff shook his head. It was a bad bet at best. He didn't think that Mac-Adoo was foolish enough to beeline it towards his plains hideout. Undoubtedly they would lay a trail in a false direction and then veer off under cover of the rain. Ruff would have. Anyone with any plains canny would.

Still, it was all they could do. "All right, Reggie. Let's do it."

At sundown the rain was light. There was no sign at all of the three bandits. No sign that any living man had ever passed this way. But some had. And recently.

They stopped on top of a low rise as sundown was filtering through the gray clouds, spreading an eerie reddish light across the plains.

"Jesus!" Reggie said, almost with reverence.

"How many?"

Reggie just shook his head. There, not a mile off, was the largest Sioux camp Ruff had ever seen. Basking in the faint sunset stood perhaps five hundred tipis. The rain moved in again and screened them off from the war camp.

"Ta-Shaka," Reggie guessed.

Ruff nodded his agreement. "At least we know Mac-Adoo didn't come this way. Let's get ourselves lost in this rain," Ruff said. Wordlessly then they rode northward, giving the Sioux village wide berth.

Ruff rode with his rifle across the saddlebows. From here on they could expect Sioux warriors at any time. There were bound to be skirmishing parties out. He thought vaguely that the army should be informed of the location of Ta-Shaka's camp, but he wasn't ready to turn back from his pursuit in order to do that.

Things were getting very complicated indeed. Trying to find the MacAdoo gang in this broad land with the storm settling in was nearly impossible. Add a band of warring Sioux and the game became one no gambler would quote odds on.

They had ridden a mile before Ruff spoke.

"You don't have to stick this, Reggie. It's getting hairy out here."

Reggie, amazingly, laughed. "What do you wish me to do, old boy? Ride back and warm my feet in the pub? Among my cherished pals? No," he said, "I'll ride with you, Mr. Justice. Jove! I'm beginning to get the feel of this bloody land again—and I'm beginning to like it."

They spent the night in a cave cut into the banks of the Chicha Coulee, a hidden spot recalled by the Arik from his childhood. They found old buffalo bones and a pottery shard in the cave, and Reggie turned these things over in his hands, perhaps reliving some faint memory.

All he said was, "It was a terrible life, old man. Dreadful and hard and uncertain. Yet one supposes there was something magnificent about it all." His voice fell off and his eyes seemed far away. Ruff left him to his reveries.

After eating they talked. "There must be some shelter out here, Reggie. Some old soddy, maybe a dugout, a cave . . . somewhere for MacAdoo to hole up. I can't see him sleeping out for month after month. The question is, where? You know the territory."

"I *did*, old chap," Reggie said, running his hand across his carefully brushed hair. "But much has changed."

"Not the land itself."

"No? It does change, Mr. Justice. These hollows . . ." He waved a hand around the shallow, firelit cave. "It doesn't take long for a river to carve such a formation out of the soft earth. A shelter . . . if it is a sod house or some such, the Sioux will have razed it, or they will have it on their agenda. Perhaps, as you suggest, a cave. There are many along the Heart River, but that is possibly too far south now to be considered."

"Too near the Sioux camp, unless MacAdoo is as mad

as Tom Dukes thought. Of course, I suppose he could have circled wide enough to come back and meet the Heart again."

"If only we knew which direction he was going." Reggie thumped the heel of his hand against his temple, trying to shake a thought free.

"We can eliminate west," Ruff thought. "Since that was the direction he was leading us."

"I think so too." Reggie was silent, his eyebrows drawn together in an effort of concentration. Then he sighed loudly, slapping his thigh.

"What is it?"

"Some elusive memory, Mr. Justice. Some thought trying to work its way to the surface."

"It'll come back to you."

"I sincerely hope so." He looked at Ruff across the tiny fire which curled smoke up against the ceiling of the cave, a ceiling blackened by the fires of centuries. Here and there people had scratched stick figures on the wall. They seemed to move in the flickering light. "I sincerely hope so, Mr. Justice, because I am almost afraid that without some sort of inspiration we haven't a chance in the world of ever laying eyes on Mr. MacAdoo and Mr. Slaussen again."

It was still raining in the morning, a light gray drizzle slanting downward, gathering in rivulets to rush toward the already swollen prairie streams.

Twice that morning Ruff and Reggie had to detour wide after crossing the tracks of large parties of Sioux or Cheyenne warriors—all riding south by west, toward the camp of the blood-mad war leader, Ta-Shaka. Trouble was coming, and it was going to be big trouble. He already had the numbers he needed to make a mockery of the strength of Fort Lincoln if it came to an open prairie war. In the meantime all traffic on the plains was held at bay, lines of communication and supply cut, every man bold enough or insane enough to wander into this zone in danger of prompt, horrible death.

"Damn my eyes!" Lord Reggie said again. They had

been criss-crossing the area, sticking to the coulees and lowland, eyes always alert to the sudden appearance of a war party. They had found, for their troubles, nothing.

"A man had any sense he'd turn back, Reggie."

"I suppose," the Arik answered with a sigh. Neither of them had any intention of doing that.

Still riding north, they intercepted the wagon train that afternoon.

Ruff held up his hand and sat waiting in the silver mist and cool gusting wind as Reggie rode up to him, his stocky pony rain-slick and weary.

"There they are," Ruff said, inclining his head. "The future dead."

"Near future," Reggie agreed, removing his cold pipe to spit. "Want to talk to them again?"

"Not much, but they're in our path and it can't hurt. Maybe it'll sink in."

With that faint hope they rode down the long grassy slope beneath the gray, moving skies and angled toward the plodding wagon train.

They had eight wagons and six outriders, three on either side. They were all armed with rifles and had the look of sodbusters. They wore, to a man, coveralls and flop hats, black rain slickers and clodhoppers.

Ruff saw the head of the near man come around, saw his mouth open as if he would yell a warning, but he didn't. He slowed the Missouri mule he rode and watched with narrowing eyes as Ruff and the Indian approached the wagon train.

"Ruff Justice," he said by way of introduction. The farmer nodded without responding. "This is Reggie Smythe. Where's Waters?"

"Fust wagon," the man finally drawled. A bony finger lifted toward the head of the train, and Ruff, touching his hatbrim with his hand, moved slowly forward past the line of creaking, heavily laden wagons.

At the second wagon he met Brent Shaughnessy. His broad, angry face came around sharply and he glared at Ruff with cutting eyes.

"What in hell are you doing here? Come crawling back for that job, have you? It's taken already, by a man with some nerve!"

"Good afternoon to you too," Ruff said. His eyes were already on someone else. Her head emerged from the rear of the covered wagon in front of Shaughnessy's. Abigail Shaughnessy.

"Afternoon, Miss Abigail," Ruff said, touching his hat-brim again. Shaughnessy uttered an animal growl, and Ruff looked at him again.

"Keep your eyes off her. Stay away from her."

Ruff nodded noncommittally and moved ahead, Reggie following. Caleb Waters was working hard guiding the six oxen he had harnessed to his wagon. He was concentrating so much and doing so poorly that Ruff knew the man had done little of this. The oxen, no matter what encouragement Caleb Waters gave them, moved forward steadily, heads bobbing, choosing their own pace. Waters cursed slowly, thickly, and then as his head turned toward Ruff, a sort of squeak rose up in his throat and died in a whispering oath.

"What do you want? Where did you come from, Justice?"

"We've been riding down south a ways, Mr. Waters." Ruff noticed the dark-eyed Abigail peering over her father's shoulder. Her lips were parted in a smile of definite welcome. "There's a big Sioux camp not twenty miles from here. Must be, oh, maybe a thousand men there."

"And more arriving," Reggie added. Waters looked at Reggie as if he had found him under a rock.

"What are you talking about? My scout has informed us quite definitely that there are no Sioux within a hundred miles. And those are to the north, camped along the Knife River, probably heading for Canada to join the rest of the renegades."

"Your scout's got holes in his skull."

"You're a liar!" Waters erupted. "There's something fishy about you, Justice. Why are you so damned set on keeping this wagon train from getting to Grizzly?"

"Because the way I hear it there is no town of Grizzly!" Ruff said. The rain was in his eyes, and he wiped it angrily away. "Because I happen to know for a fact that there's five or six hundred Sioux—minimum—within a day's ride of here and *they know you're here.*"

"Not likely," Waters said. Still, there was a shadow of worry in his eyes. Ruff felt sorry for the man in a vague way. He didn't read Caleb Waters for bad man, just a stubborn one trying desperately to make his contract good, to save his bets. The trouble was he was betting his daughter's life and those of the sodbusters who had agreed to travel with him.

"It's true." Ruff explained briefly about the fight with the Sioux, about the one who got away. Waters just shook his head negatively, heavily, as if it weighed a ton.

"I can't accept this, not from you."

"Will you let me talk to your guide?" Ruff asked. "Who is he? Where is he?"

"I can't see what—"

"Where is he?" Ruff demanded.

"Mr. Curtis is a half a day ahead of us."

"Half a day! In these conditions?" Ruff glanced at Reggie, who could only shake his head.

"He wanted to make sure that the trail was clear, that the ford at Grand Coulee wasn't washed out, that there were no Sioux—" Waters held up a hand, "I know, I know, but he's a cautious man. He doesn't believe there are any out there, but he wants to be sure. He's a thorough man."

"I want to talk to him." Ruff's eyes lifted to the trail ahead. "If he manages to get back alive, that is."

"What in hell's going on?" The voice was Brent Shaughnessy's, audible above the plodding of the oxen, the creaking and groaning of the wagons, the patter of the rain. Ruff glanced at Abigail, who smiled again and vanished.

"Worries a lot about his wife," Justice said.

"And my daughter!" Waters objected, knowing what Ruff meant.

"What's this Curtis's other name? It doesn't ring a bell with me."

"Averill, I believe. Yes, Averill Curtis." Waters frowned, paused to curse the oxen, which he stung with a long-handled whip, producing no visible effect. "I can't see what business it is of yours." After a moment's consideration he asked, "What are you doing out here anyway, if it's so unsafe?"

"Damned if I know," Ruff said with a grin. "I'm damned if I know, Waters. Still, I want to talk to your guide. If I can convince him, if I can show him the Sioux camp, then will you turn back?"

"Well . . ." Waters was hesitant. His face drew itself downward. He shook his head again. "Perhaps . . . yes, I suppose I would have no choice."

"Then I'll wait for him. He comes in for supper, I suppose?"

"Yes, yes, of course."

"I'll talk to you, then. Good day, Mr. Waters." Ruff slowed his gray and let the lurching wagon draw on past. After the second in line, driven by the murderous-looking Brent Shaughnessy, had gone by, Ruff asked:

"Have you ever heard of a man named Averill Curtis, Reggie?"

"Never have. Of course, I've been away."

"I haven't. Not for that long. Anybody fit to guide a wagon train across the plains, I'd know of him."

"It doesn't follow that the man is qualified for the job just because he landed it, old man," Reggie pointed out.

"That's what worries me. He's proved he *isn't* qualified. Why a half day ahead of the train, Reggie? Does that make any sense to you at all?"

"Not to me, sport. But then I'll never understand you Yanks," he said with the barest of yawns. Ruff grinned, slapped him on the shoulder, and together they rode on, keeping to the rear of the train.

"You still haven't described Grange and Crowder to me," Ruff reminded him.

"I was afraid you'd ride off and leave me, Mr. Justice.

Nobly, I'm sure, not wanting old Reggie to get his own scalp taken out here." He settled into the saddle, using both hands to gesture. "Crowder you can't miss if you see him. He's narrow, with a broken nose which forms an S across his face. Ring finger missing—they say he lost a ruby ring in a poker game and Crowder couldn't get it off so the winner applied a Bowie to the problem. Embittered Crowder, and he applied a similar weapon to the malefactor's throat. Oh—he's also as bald as an egg."

He would be difficult to miss, Ruff reflected. Grange was going to be more difficult.

"He's a big man, not fat. Medium complexion. I don't know what color his hair is, or his eyes. I only know one remarkable fact which could identify him. As a boy he was caught raiding a vegetable patch and was shot with a load of rock salt. He's said"—Reggie lifted an amused eyebrow—"to have a thoroughly pockmarked pair of buttocks."

"That's fine—all we have to do is ask every man we meet to drop his pants for us." Still, Ruff was grinning. He wasn't worried a lot about Grange. It was MacAdoo and Slaussen who were the big game, and likely Grange was with one or the other.

He was more concerned with who and what Averill Curtis was. He was soon to find out, painfully.

7

NIGHTTIME FOUND THE skies bright, patched with woolly, exhausted clouds. A cold wind bent the red cones of fire. The wagons had been drawn up in a circle—for all the good that would do against such numbers as Ruff had seen.

Some intelligent person had a smoked ham turning over one fire, and the smells drifted temptingly through the air. Ruff and Reggie sat apart, finishing off the cold beans and acrid coffee.

"Those fires don't help," Reggie commented.

"They don't hurt—Ta-Shaka already knows exactly where this outfit is located. He's just taking his time."

"Have you talked to any of these people?" Reggie asked. He lifted his chin. The sodbusters gathered around the fire were lean and determined men, their women capable and grim.

"What's the point in it now?" Ruff asked. "We must be at midpoint. It's as far back to Bismarck as it is to Grizzly. Either direction is deadly now."

"I say!" Reggie leaned back on an elbow, the damp grass enveloping him. "Is that our boy?" His dark finger was extended toward the far side of the wagon circle. Someone was coming in. The guide?

Ruff rose and picked up his hat. "I thought you said it was too late to turn back anyway," Reggie said.

"Probably. But we could veer north, get out of Ta-Shaka's path. Besides, I want to see what kind of son of a bitch would lead these people out here."

"Restraint, old man," Reggie said with a grin. "Probably just another poor soul trying to make a living any way he can."

Ruff didn't answer. He turned and walked across the camp, a tall, long-legged man with a drooping mustache and cold blue eyes. The settlers, perhaps believing themselves secure within the flimsy protection of their ringed wagons, looked up and remarked his passing. Waters must have spoken to some of them, for the looks were not all simply curious, many were downright hostile.

Seeing a stout woman in blue gingham nursing an infant, Ruff winced.

There were other children with the wagon train. All shapes and sizes. They were bright-eyed and eager. Traveling toward their new homes, homes they would never reach, and Ruff felt an anger stirring.

Anger with Waters, with this guide, Averill Curtis, with himself—the man who was going to leave them here to be butchered. He was riding a vengeance trail, seeking to kill those who had torn his heart out. But what of the little ones, the women, the hardworking sodbusters? What kind of man was he to ride off and leave them? Could he do it at all?

Ruff knew already he was a fool ever to have ridden into this camp.

Averill Curtis had leaped his horse over the tongue of the Waters's wagon and was now standing, hat tipped back, in close consultation with Caleb Waters. Ruff walked directly up to them, noticing the foaming mouth, the sweat-streaked flanks of Curtis's blaze-faced roan. The man had ridden a long way, and rapidly. But why?

"Hello, Mr. Waters," Ruff said, easing up next to the two men. Waters turned glassy eyes on Justice.

"Hello, Mr. Justice. This is Averill Curtis—I believe you've been waiting to speak with him."

"I have. Evening, Mr. Curtis."

Ruff didn't extend his hand, and Curtis didn't offer his. Curtis was broad-shouldered, lean in the hips, with an odd, pale cast to his seemingly colorless eyes. He wore half boots, a fringed vest, and a narrow-brimmed hat which had once been white. He also had a Colt hung at fingertip length and a long-barreled Sharps .50 caliber. The horse shuddered and blew, breaking the odd moment of silence.

"Heard of you," Curtis said slowly. His upper lip tended to curl back of its own volition, showing irregular white teeth.

"That right? Funny I've never heard of *you*," Ruff responded. Curtis didn't like that much.

"Mr. Justice is concerned," Waters put in hastily. "He reports many Sioux warriors not far south of us. He claims they know where we are."

"Nonsense," Curtis said easily. "I'm telling you they're far north. The road into Grizzly is clear—"

"And the town is prospering," Ruff said.

"That's right," Curtis answered slowly. His eyes hardened. "What's it to you, friend?"

"Nothing. Except I don't believe you." Curtis stiffened. You didn't call a man a liar in this part of the country, not without expecting trouble. But Justice, damn him, was grinning. "I've heard that Grizzly is deserted," he went on, looking at Waters and not the guide.

"Did you?" Curtis laughed, but it sounded forced to Ruff Justice. "Well, it ain't. I was in sight of it this afternoon. Business as usual, it looked like. People in the streets, wagons moving to the digs east of town."

Ruff was stumped. He could call the man a liar—maybe he was, but his only source of information had been a half-drunk prospector gabbling in a saloon back in Bismarck. If Curtis had actually been near the town, had actually seen . . . why couldn't he believe that?

"I'm getting mighty hungry, Mr. Waters," Curtis said, removing his hat to wipe the sweat band. "Justice, I've got no quarrel with you. There's a misunderstanding somewhere, that's all. If you're going to stay, I'd be

71

obliged to have you ride with me, help out. If you're leaving, well, I hope it's with no hard feelings. Sorry we got off on the wrong foot."

Then he thrust out his hand, and Ruff had no choice but to take it. Curtis's hand was dry, strong, and nearly friendly, but there was reserve on his lips, and his eyes were positively cold.

"Oh, there you are!" The voice was feminine, intriguing, and Ruff turned, expecting to see what he did see—Abigail Shaughnessy walking toward them, her hips swaying from side to side in primordial invitation. What he did not expect was for the woman to walk directly to him and kiss him on the mouth, her lips parting, her tongue flickering over his lips, her breasts pressed flat against his chest, her hands clenching his back passionately for a fragment of a minute before she stepped back and Ruff was caught in the knifelike glare of Caleb Waters.

Curtis's reaction was more unexpected. He stepped forward, jaw clenched, and for a minute Ruff thought that the guide was going to have a shot at him. Just as suddenly as she had begun it, Abigail ended it. She stepped back, a mocking half-smile on her lips, turned on a dainty heel, and walked away, vanishing in the campfire-cast shadows.

Ruff had only time to turn at the sound of the approaching footsteps, time to recognize the savagely distorted face of Brent Shaughnessy before the man's shoulder slammed into his chest and they went down in a tumbling mass of arms and legs, thudding against the wagon wheel behind Ruff, sending Curtis's horse rearing away in panic.

Ruff had no time to block the first sledgehammer blow Shaughnessy winged at his head, and it caught him high on the temple, setting the bells to ringing, the lights to flickering inside his skull.

He kicked out savagely and heard Shaughnessy grunt, and he came to his feet in time to meet a wildly thrown left hook. Ruff partially blocked the blow with his forearm, but still it stung, catching him on the point of the chin, driving him back against the wagon bed.

Men were rushing toward the scene of the fight. A woman screamed. Ruff saw it all only subconsciously; his concentration was focused on the big blond man before him. The man was red-faced, wide-eyed. The cords of his neck stood out tautly. His fists were bunched into balls hanging at his sides.

He was white-knuckled and wild with fury. He was mad enough to kill in this jealous rage, and Ruff had a moment to wonder if that wasn't exactly what the lovely Abigail had had in mind before Brent Shaughnessy lunged forward with a roar.

Ruff ducked an overhand right and countered with his own jolting uppercut to Shaughnessy's wind. He found hard muscle beneath that bulky gut of Shaughnessy's. The man was nearly lifted from his feet with the force of the uppercut, but it didn't slow him appreciably.

He was big and clumsy and mad as hell, and he bored in on Ruff Justice.

He lurched forward, pinning Ruff to the side of the wagon. The first right hand missed, and Shaughnessy yowled with pain as his fist slammed into the wagon bed. There was no time for Ruff to be amused by the miss.

The second right was a triphammer punch which caught Justice on the ribs, knocking the breath from him, causing his legs to buckle momentarily.

Ruff covered up and twisted free, trading places with Shaughnessy. He had the big man against the wagon now, and he fired three rapid lefts into the big man's face, spraying them both with blood as Shaughnessy's nose caved in.

Shaughnessy half turned away and lifted a knee, trying for Ruff's groin, but the tall man had been expecting it, and he crossed a leg over, blocking the knee, which landed painfully on his thigh.

He stepped back, trying to give himself room to fight, but Shaughnessy was all over him, his breath wheezing out in tight gasps as he rained blows on Justice. Many of them missed altogether, but the few that landed were stunning, and Justice reeled.

Shaughnessy had the strength of an insane man, and just then he was insane, mad with jealousy. He came forward, and Ruff, sidestepping, aimed a kick at Shaughnessy's knee, trying to disable the man. He missed just enough. Shaughnessy plowed ahead.

A left jarred Ruff, and a right dug into his ribs again. The pain was excruciating, and Ruff wondered fleetingly if a rib hadn't cracked.

He backed away, jabbing at the big man's head, watching it bob with each solid blow he landed, but it didn't slow Shaughnessy down. Nothing did.

Ruff was backed against the tongue of Waters's wagon, and it caught him in back of the knees. He tried to move forward, but a shove, an open-handed blow to his chest, sent him toppling over it and onto the hard ground.

Shaughnessy flung himself through the air, diving on Ruff, who managed to get his leg up in time to send the big man flying past to land at a bad angle, twisting his neck. It didn't slow Shaughnessy.

He got to his feet, shaking his head like a stunned ox. Then, mammoth arms spread, he came in again, slipping his hands around Ruff before Justice could evade him.

The arms tightened around him in a big bear hug, the grip like iron bands. Ruff could feel himself starting to go, the ribs and spine popping as the deadly grip tightened still more. He threw his head back in anguish and jammed the heel of his hand against Shaughnessy's damaged nose.

The big man grunted and turned his head aside, burying his face against Ruff's chest. The grip only grew stronger. Cartilage crackled; his lungs, empty now, were on fire. His head spun with the lack of oxygen.

Wildly Ruff fought back, slamming the side of his fist against the side of Shaughnessy's neck. In a fury the big man lifted Ruff even higher and then slammed him to the earth.

Ruff landed awkwardly. His head grazed the tongue of the wagon, but he was free. Free and nearly as mad now as Shaughnessy. He moved in, throwing stinging punches with left and right hands, backing the blond man away.

Shaughnessy caught a right to the wind, grunted, and moved to the side only to catch a left coming in squarely on the jaw. Ruff's long hair was in his face now. Blood stained his shirt—his or Shaughnessy's. Perhaps both. He had the man backing away, and he meant to keep him off balance, back on his heels, and so he forged ahead, throwing crisp rights and lefts to the puzzled face of Brent Shaughnessy.

The big man was tiring badly now. His onslaught had accomplished little except to leave him arm-weary. Now, the first surge of anger dying away, he felt exhausted and, it seemed, puzzled. The man had not gone down under his barrage of fists. Far from it—Justice had gotten his balance and his second wind. His muscles, pumped full of hot blood now, responded to his mind's quick impulses, and the battered Shaughnessy could only retreat as a left caught the shelf of his jaw, caught it again, and the big man staggered, putting out a hand to brace himself should he fall.

But he didn't go down, not that easily. Shaughnessy was a big and powerful man, yet he had to spin away, to cover his face with those massive forearms, satisfying himself with only an occasional ineffective counterpunch.

Ruff could see the confidence wash out of the big man's face. One wild right from Shaughnessy, thrown with all of his weight behind it, with all the leverage of shoulders and hips behind it, connected with Justice's jaw, and the man laughed—damn him!—he simply laughed and shook it off, coming in again with a series of hooks which dug at Shaughnessy's wind.

Shaughnessy, like so many big men, was a one-punch fighter, used to winning his brawls with a mauling, swarming attack. But Justice had taken his best and had not gone down. Now Shaughnessy's defense was springing leaks—and so was his composure.

They had worked their way back into the wagon circle,

the sodbusters standing gloomily aside, watching as Shaughnessy took the beating of his life.

Ruff had him backing away still. He watched and waited. One good opening, he knew, and Shaughnessy would go down.

The rifle appeared from nowhere. Tossed through the air, it was clutched in Shaughnessy's meaty hand. Ruff halted, stepped back, watched as Shaughnessy levered a cartridge into the chamber, and he spun aside, landing on the ground as the rifle spat flame. A .44-40 bullet dug a long angry furrow in the earth beside Ruff, and he palmed his Colt, coming to his feet as Shaughnessy worked desperately at the lever of the Henry repeater, which had inexplicably become jammed.

Ruff moved in, seeing Shaughnessy's face go pale, seeing his eyes widen and settle on the deadly blue steel Colt in Justice's hand.

"No . . . Justice! No . . ." he managed to stutter before Ruff stepped in.

Grasping the barrel of the rifle with one hand, Ruff jerked, and as Shaughnessy, off-balance, lurched toward him, Ruff hammered down with his Colt, slamming the barrel against Shaughnessy's skull, opening a long scarlet gash above the big man's eye. He went down like a pole-axed steer.

Justice stood there, rifle in one hand, Colt in the other, looking over the gathered settlers, Caleb Waters, gray and grim, the expressionless Averill Curtis, the full-breasted, dark-eyed Abigail Shaughnessy, who stood to one side, arms folded, lips amused, and finally he looked down at the peacefully sleeping man at his feet, at the battered bloody face of Brent Shaughnessy. Flinging the rifle away, he turned and walked away from the wagons, his heart hammering, his legs weaker than he would have wanted them to know.

"I did recommend restraint," Reginald Darby-Smythe said, putting a supporting arm around Ruff's waist.

"He didn't make it easy," Ruff replied. Each breath was painful, and now that the fight was done his body seemed to go slack, to nudge him here and there with complaints.

Reggie had laid out their bedrolls some distance from the wagon train, and as he helped Ruff to a sitting position he stood over him and asked: "Anything that needs attending to?"

"I don't think so. I'm all in one piece, just a little loosely strung together. Give me a cup of coffee, will you, Reggie?"

"It's cold."

"It doesn't matter." Ruff accepted the tin cup of bitter, dark liquid and then, with a blanket across his shoulders, he sat hunched forward, staring at the wagons.

"Makes you wonder what that was about, doesn't it, old man? A bit much over nothing in particular."

"It does, Reggie. It does make a man wonder." He was silent, thoughtful for a minute.

"It was the woman who caused it," Ruff said finally. "Deliberately, calculatingly."

"Yes?" Reggie lifted an eyebrow. He was crouched beside Ruff, his arms dangling between his legs. A pale half-moon had shaken free of the clouds and it shone now across the damp, grassy land, lending an eerie sheen to the low hills. "Maybe she simply couldn't resist your animal magnetism, old boy."

"She could have resisted it for a few minutes more," Ruff said sourly. But maybe Reggie was right—there were women that impetuous, and Ruff had met some. Maybe, too, she had simply wanted to anger her husband, to get even with him—Ruff had run into a few of that kind as well, deadly with their little games.

"I think there's something else to it," he told the Indian.

"Any ideas?"

"Not really. All I know is that she wanted that fight to happen. She instigated it."

"Unless she didn't know Shaughnessy was around. Could be she believed him asleep or busy at his chores," Reggie suggested.

"Still . . . it was right under her father's eyes."

"To discredit you with Caleb Waters?" Reggie asked, shrugging. "Why then, Ruff?"

"I don't know, *old boy*," Ruff said, smiling. "I just don't know, but I wish to God I did. I've got the feeling that it might make all the difference."

They didn't talk anymore. Ruff rolled up in his bed, watching the moon for a long while, listening to the calling of an owl. The fires slowly burned out in the circle of wagons below them.

Why? What in the hell had Abigail Shaughnessy been thinking of? Maybe Reggie was right—she was just a hot-blooded, beautiful woman used to doing what she wanted, when and where she wanted, the consequences be damned. Somehow Ruff didn't think so.

Matters were getting too complicated altogether. There were MacAdoo and Slaussen, the Sioux and the Cheyenne. This scout Curtis, who seemed to be leading them deliberately into a massacre. And now this.

A man with any brains would ride out now, at least in the morning, leaving the whole bunch of them to suffer what they deserved, but there were the women down there, and kids, innocents sucked into this . . . what?

What exactly was going on here, anyhow? Was it only Caleb Waters's greed which drove this band of people on toward their deaths? What was behind those dark eyes, that sensual, kiss-me smile of Abigail Shaughnessy?

It was all too much on this night. Ruff rolled up more snugly in his blankets and tried to sleep, his body stiffening now, jolting him awake with prodding fingers of pain.

Still, he did manage to sleep, uneasily, until sometime around midnight, when the warm, naked woman slipped into his bedroll.

8

SHE CAME INTO his bed, and even in his present condition when aching muscles and savaged cartilage cried out for rest, demanded to be left untouched, the curve and heft of her warm body against his was enough to start the blood racing through his veins, to cause his heart to lift to an excited pacing, to bring the loins to slow, pulsing eagerness.

She was soft and her thigh was a warm miracle against his leg, her breasts pendulous and firm, demanding attentive caresses. Her lips were gentle and pliant, finding his mouth and searching it diligently, each gentle touch stirring him more.

He was dreaming, had to be. He opened his eyes, and his sleep-blurred vision, the pale moon backlighting her, made her appear blond and familiar.

There was something about the touch, however, something about the hands, which seemed grasping, unfamiliar, as they ran up his thigh and hefted him, stirring him. Louise was dead!

"Abigail."

"Who else, darling?" She bent lower, kissing his throat, and his hands rose with the involuntary instinct in every man to find her breasts, to cup them, to toy with the taut nipples. She kissed him again, and then he felt her breath on his ear. Moist, rapid, eager.

"Hold it. What is all this?" He held her shoulders, looking up into those moon-glossed eyes, and she laughed deep in her throat.

"What is it? What does it look like? It's you, Ruff Justice. I've been mad for you since I laid eyes on you. I want you all over me, in me, I need you."

"And Brent?"

"You don't have to worry about my husband. He's sleeping like a stone." She laughed again, even more softly, more evilly it seemed. "Besides, he wouldn't come at you again, darling, not after what you did to him."

"No?" Ruff's mouth was overwhelmed by her lips again. She was tender, warm, and alluring in the night—a compelling creature, was Mrs. Abigail Shaughnessy. Ruff would have to have been less than human not to respond to her kisses, her pouting encouragements, the graze of her hand against his thighs, her whispered endearments, and Ruff Justice was hardly less than human—not when it came to naked women in his bed, women who undid his shirt and slipped warm hands inside of it to touch his chest and slide down across his abdomen, seeking him.

But he hadn't been raised a fool either. The woman was sly, and perhaps just now she was overestimating herself.

Still, he couldn't help drawing her down to him, couldn't help pressing his body flat against hers, feeling the quiver which ran through her, the sudden slackness of her, the tremors as he ran his lips across the soft mounds of her breasts, full, almost arrogant in the moonlight. He couldn't help letting his hand run up between her thighs and meet the soft welcome there. . . .

"Not here, not here," she said urgently, squirming away. She lifted her chin toward Reggie and said, "In my wagon. Brent's angry with me. He's not there and he won't be back."

"Abigail . . ."

"Fifteen minutes. Give me a minute to get there and get ready. Fifteen minutes, Mr. Justice." She leaned toward him, kissed him hungrily one last time, and then was gone, wrapping a heavy blanket around herself as she scurried across the night-blackened grass and vanished.

"That is a lot of woman," Reggie said from his bed. His eyes were still closed, but he was smiling.

"Definitely."

"I couldn't help listening."

"Jealous?"

"Naturally," Reggie said. "Are you going down there?"

"Not on your life, Reggie."

"The poor lady—she'll suffer such disappointment."

"Go on down yourself," Ruff suggested lightly.

"Uh-uh. Not on your life, as a friend of mine has remarked. There's something crooked about that lady. But, God, Justice—she's almost enough to make it worth while."

"Almost," Ruff agreed.

But not quite. Ruff rolled over, wondering. His body slowly cooled and the fever in his brain died down. Still, if he tried, he could imagine the closeness of her body, the ripe competentness of it, the eager lips, the slow swelling of her breasts . . . he tried not to imagine it, and even that wasn't much help.

"Ruff."

Reggie's voice was a whisper, and Justice opened one eye. "What is it?"

"Something funny. Abigail—I could swear it was her. She went away from the wagons. Look there."

Ruff sat up cautiously and peered into the darkness. "I don't see a thing."

"There's a clump of boulders. There—see her moving by the rocks?"

Ruff did see a vague, shadowy movement, but he couldn't make out what she was doing. After a minute she shook herself free of the shadows and hurried back toward the wagon.

"She's dressed now," Reggie pointed out. "Must have given up on you, sport."

"Must have. Or maybe . . ." Ruff's comment was interrupted by a piercing, hysterical scream. They jumped to their feet, guns in hand, and saw Abigail Shaughnessy leap from the back of her wagon, saw men rushing toward her. And she screamed and screamed again.

Justice was on the move already, loping down the slope, his eyes flickering to the shadows and back to the group of people gathered at the rear of the Shaughnessy wagon.

Someone had started a fire, and three or four torches were thrust into the flames and rushed to the scene of activity.

Caleb was there, and his daughter clung to him. People were asking a dozen questions at once. Justice was suddenly into the circle of firelight, and eyes stabbed out toward him, lost interest, and returned to the woman who stood shuddering, sobbing hysterically in her father's arms.

Waters was murmuring soft reassurances to his daughter, and then his voice rose abruptly as she gurgled something to him.

"We'll see about that! By God . . . he deserved it!" Caleb Waters thundered. He shoved past Ruff and half a dozen others to enter the rear of the Shaughnessy wagon. Ruff followed him up.

The torches blazed away behind him, and as Ruff stepped up into the wagon a lantern flared to life.

Waters tried to bar Ruff from entering the wagon, from seeing what lay crumpled on the bed, but it was too late. He was already up; he had already seen the bloody, dead figure of Averill Curtis, seen the knife protruding from his back, seen Brent Shaughnessy, his face still puffed and purple from the fistfight, sitting on the edge of a chair, his big hands dangling between his legs—hands which were soaked with blood.

Behind Ruff a big man with a head which should have belonged to a buffalo softly muttered, "Jesus!"

"He went crazy," Abigail was saying. Her eyes were brimming with tears. The scout wasn't able to reply to that, so Abigail went on, hovering over the bloody form like a fluttering angel. She waved her hands and went on.

"I was waiting for Brent to come back from supper—you know how late we all ate this evening—and when Mr. Curtis came in I assumed he wanted to speak to Brent as well."

Curious heads poked into the wagon, looked at the blood-spattered floor and canvas top, at the still, twisted body of Averill Curtis, and exchanged muttered comments.

Abigail swallowed, touched her nose with a small, lacy handkerchief, and went on, "When I told him he was welcome to wait for Brent, he simply grinned. He came at me . . ." Abigail looked up and caught Ruff Justice's eyes on her. She flinched slightly, and then those watery eyes sparked angrily.

"Go on, honey, what happened?" her father encouraged. Brent Shaughnessy still hadn't moved. He sat like an overgrown dejected schoolboy in the corner, his heavy face immobile.

"He came at me and grabbed me! He was pawing at me . . ." There was a decent pause while Abigail collected herself, hiding her face briefly in the lace hanky.

"Brent came in?" her father prompted.

"Yes." She gripped her father's arm tightly, looking up at him with helpless eyes. "Brent found him and . . . well, you know Brent's temper. He stabbed him . . . he couldn't have even been thinking about what he was doing." She lifted her eyes to the gathered men. "He was only trying to protect me!"

"Don't you worry about it," the man with the mournful buffalo head replied. "A man's got the right to defend wife and home. Nothin's going to happen to your husband."

"Hell no," another sodbuster said in agreement. "I'd've done the same."

"So would I. Any of us would. Come on, Henry, give me a hand gettin' this body out of here."

"Hold on a minute," Ruff said, placing his hand on the sodbuster's wrist as he started to step up.

"What are you interfering for, Justice? You heard the lady. Let us get that bastard out of here."

"I think," Ruff said, "we ought to hear what Mr. Shaughnessy has to say."

"Why? We know what happened. Or would you like it if we took Shaughnessy out and hung him?"

"Get out of the way, Justice," Caleb Waters snapped. The old man appeared drawn and weary.

"I want to hear Shaughnessy's story."

Waters sighed and slapped his thighs with his palms. "All right. Christ! Brent, what happened?"

Shaughnessy lifted his head and fixed brooding eyes on Ruff Justice. "It's like Abigail says. I found 'im. I killed 'im."

"Satisfied?" Buffalo Head said sourly.

"No. Not quite," Ruff answered.

"Come on, Justice!" Waters practically moaned. "What the hell are you after? We've heard the story. We believe them. What is it that's bothering you?"

"The lies." Ruff smiled thinly. "Look here, Waters—this man was stabbed. Cut a big artery when the knife went in. Take a look at the blood spattered around in here." Ruff lifted a pointing finger. "All up the canvas, across the bed of the wagon. Now look at Shaughnessy."

"There's blood on him, sure. What are you getting at, Justice?"

"There's blood on his *hands*. Nowhere else. That's what I'm getting at. Whoever did this should be drenched with the stuff."

Ruff looked at Abigail again, and her eyes, black as coals, sparking with emotion, met his. Her jaw was clenched, her lips compressed until they were white.

"What are you saying?"

"I'm saying that these two are lying," Justice said easily.

"You mean Shaughnessy didn't do it? Then why? Why concoct a story to protect someone else? And who else could it have been, come to that?" Waters was trembling with anger. Ruff answered him coolly.

"It was Abigail that did it," Ruff said.

Shaughnessy launched himself from his chair and stood, chest heaving, before Ruff, his lumpy face distorted still more by anger. "You saying I'm lying? You saying my wife murdered this man?"

Ruff turned away from him. "Abigail left this wagon a little while ago. She was out near that clump of boulders to the north. I'd like to know what she was doing there."

"I can't see . . ." Waters sputtered.

"I can," Buffalo Head said. "Let's have a look, Carl. Somebody bring a torch."

Feeling the eyes boring holes in his back, Ruff slid down to the ground and joined the procession walking toward the jumbled boulders to the north of the camp. They found it.

"Look here," Buffalo Head said heavily. He held up the gingham dress, dark with blood. His toe prodded a bundle of long buffalo grass used to wipe bloody hands. "What do we do now?"

He was looking at Caleb Waters, who was supporting his daughter as if he expected her to faint away. Abigail was made of sterner stuff. Her face, glossed with firelight, was set and hard, a wax mask. Her eyes glittered, looking evilly at Ruff Justice, who stood, his weight on one foot, watching her.

"I'll not see a woman hung," the man named Carl said.

"No," Buffalo Head said evenly. "Nor will I. There's nothing to do except hold her for the law in Grizzly. Mr. Waters?"

"I have nothing to say. I don't believe any of this. It's some sort of trick Justice has planned for us."

No one swallowed that. They trudged back toward the wagon circle, Ruff watching the slim-waisted, broad-hipped woman being led before him, wondering . . . wondering if a trap set for him had somehow gone wrong.

Abigail had come hunting him. She had invited him to her wagon that evening. In the darkness there could have been a mistake. Maybe Averill Curtis had taken the knife meant for Ruff himself.

"We're without a guide," Carl reminded them all. "Unless . . ." His eyes drifted to those of Justice, who made no response.

"I don't like any of this," Buffalo Head said morosely. He had reason to be unhappy. In hostile territory, they now had a murderess on their hands. Worst of all, she had killed the one man whose responsibility was to lead them through the Sioux-infested country to Grizzly.

Reaching the wagon, they drew up in an uncertain half circle. Brent Shaughnessy still stood in the wagon, feet planted on the tailgate, as he had been when they left him.

"Well?" he asked, and they told him. He only nodded slowly and turned away. Ruff supposed the big dumb bastard did love this woman. Probably she had told him that same story—Averill Curtis had attacked her. She had had to stab him. She was frightened. And he had backed her up.

Justice was to the tailgate again, stepping up, when Caleb Waters demanded, "Haven't you done enough! It's over. What are you up to now?"

Justice ignored him. He ducked his head and entered the covered wagon. Shaughnessy had returned to his chair, looking beat and exhausted.

Ruff walked to the corpse, rolled it over, undid the belt, and rolled it back. Then, as they watched him with uncomprehending eyes, he tugged Curtis's pants off.

The man's buttocks shone in the lanternlight. They were literally riddled with hundreds of irregular pock-marks.

"Justice, damn you," Waters screamed, "have you no decency!" He halted abruptly, looking down. "What in God's name caused something like that?"

"Rock salt," Ruff said without looking up. He covered the man's ass. "This guide of yours—his name was Grange. He's a notorious outlaw."

Waters moved his jaw several times without getting a sound out. Ruff stood and turned to Abigail, whose face was immobile.

"Well?" Justice asked. "You killed him. Did you know who he was?"

The lady apparently had nothing to say. She stood there glaring malevolently at Justice, her eyes cutting, a look that could kill, tiny soft hands which had.

Justice nodded to Buffalo Head. "Now he's yours. Take him out and bury him."

"Justice . . ." The man shook his head and clamped his jaw. "Come on, Carl. Let's get him in the ground."

Ruff walked back through the night toward his bed. The clouds had slipped past them and now covered the moon darkly, leaving only a faint silver glow where it had been.

Reggie was sitting up, arms looped around his knees. "Well?" he asked.

"Abigail Shaughnessy," Ruff told him, rolling up his bed—he wouldn't be able to sleep any more that night. "She killed Grange."

"Grange!"

"Yes. He was masquerading as Averill Curtis. Clever, in a way. Using the wagon train to make his escape."

"Why did she do it?" There was a brief flare of matchlight as Reggie got his pipe going. The tobacco smoke drifted past Ruff and was whipped away by the night breeze.

"I don't know, Reggie, and it worries me."

"Did she know who it was?"

"I've no idea. There's at least three possibilities. First, she might have thought he was me. You heard her setting me up for something. Second, she may have had a grudge against him as Averill Curtis. He may actually have gotten some idea about bedding the lady—she does come on to a man—or there may have been some reason we know nothing about. Third, she knew he was Grange. Why kill him then, I couldn't say. The possibilities are too numerous to speculate on."

"She may have been blackmailing him," Reggie said. "Or she might have demanded that he leave. Or . . ." He sighed and smiled, blowing out a stream of smoke. "He may have been strongarming her father, wanting a share of his sutlership. As you say, the possibilities are endless. You don't expect the woman to tell us, I take it?"

"I don't expect her to say a damn word, no. She'll have a plausible explanation when and if she ever goes to trial, and no doubt she'll have a husband and a father to back her up in whatever she says."

"Too bad," Reggie said, leaning back to puff contentedly at that curved pipe. "She really is an extraordinary woman, Ruff. Looking at her—well, you know what I mean."

"I know. I almost fell for it hard."

Reggie was silent then for a long while. The clouds continued their southward voyage, drifting over to clot the sky. "Well," he said eventually. "That's one down. You can notch him on your coup stick."

"Grange."

"Yes, Grange. Three to go. Say, Justice—have these people any notion at all where they are headed now? With Curtis gone, I mean?"

"I doubt it." Ruff poked at the dark earth with a twig. "I don't even think they've got sentries out right now."

"And all those women and children . . ." Reggie's voice drifted away.

"I know, dammit," Ruff said softly. "I know."

But even saying a man could get them through to Grizzly, what then? Unless the old prospector Ruff had spoken with had been cracked, there was nothing left of Grizzly—absolutely nothing. Which brought up another point—did Grange know that? If so, why was he guiding them through? Maybe the outlaw was planning on getting as far as he could with the wagon train and then simply riding off.

Last question: Why had Grange decided on this tactic? A falling-out among thieves? Why hadn't he simply ridden off with MacAdoo, Crowder, and Slaussen? Tug Slaussen. The murderous son of a bitch.

There in the darkness, in the night silence, her image came back again, those laughing green eyes, the soft corn-

88

silk golden hair, the gentle touch of Louise. And again the terrible, sudden image of the gaping hole, the white eyes, the *thing* which was not Louise lying crumpled at his feet.

"I'm taking a walk, Reggie."

"Sure. I understand perfectly, old man."

Not exactly. He couldn't understand *perfectly*. The slender quickness of her, the contours of her body when she slept, the mound of her breast, the flaring upsweep of her hip, the long dark lashes, the lithe strength of her thighs clasping . . .

Ruff walked angrily through the night. He circled the camp, seeing its vulnerability, sifting the murder of Grange and all of its various implications through his mind, resolving nothing. He sat on a rocky outcropping along the low hill to the north of the camp. Even from there he could see the two men who walked the perimeter of the wagon ring, see how vulnerable they were. The moonlight was faint, but it was enough to illuminate them distinctly, making targets of them.

Maybe, he reflected, they believed all those tales about Indians not fighting at night. He shook his head and rose, trying to dislodge the memories which clung to him like tormenting leeches.

Maybe . . .

The shot rang out as loud as thunder in the stillness of midnight, and then the war whoop, a second shot and a third, and suddenly the night was alive with fire and death.

9

THEY CAME OUT of nowhere, rising up from the dark earth like a plague of demons. Justice shouldn't have been surprised. He had been expecting something like this, but all the same the suddenness of the attack, the shrill, eerie war cries, the sudden thunder of the guns overwhelmed him for a bare moment.

The second wave of rifle fire brought him sharply to himself. The camp was under attack. Stabbing tongues of flame marked the positions of the sodbusters distinctly. Ruff hoped they were smart enough to fire and move, before enemy fire, sighting on the muzzle flashes, sought them out, but he doubted that. These weren't fighting men, they were farmers, family men, men with a special sort of courage—the kind it took to pull up roots and traverse an unknown land to search for a dream—but not soldiers.

Ruff heard a scream of pain, and he knew that with the dawn there would be a mourning widow.

He moved swiftly around the hilly area north of the camp. To rush toward the wagons and add his weapon to those already firing would accomplish nothing. He needed to be behind the enemy—to see what he was shooting at. He doubted any of the sodbusters even knew what they were aiming for.

One of the wagons had caught fire, and he heard a

woman scream, saw people tumbling out of the back of it, frantic shadows in the night.

Ruff ran on. Dipping into a gully, he ran southward, weaving around the boulders strewn along the dark creekbed. Already he knew that this was not an all-out assault by Ta-Shaka's warriors. Had it been, the train would have been overrun by now, every man, woman, and child dead.

It was likely that this was a small wandering war party—perhaps young men seeking to count coup. But there were enough of them. Plenty to overwhelm the inexperienced farmers who were defending the wagon train.

Ruff threw himself to his belly, his rifle in front of him. Not thirty yards off, three Sioux braves sat their ponies, sniping intermittently at the wagons. They were relaxed and casual about this. And why not? They were risking nothing sitting back on the hill like this. It was great fun.

It was about to get a lot less amusing.

Ruff Justice rose to his feet, staying in a deep crouch. A glance at the shadowy moon assured him that the clouds were thick enough, drifting in the proper direction so that it wouldn't suddenly burst through like a beacon.

Ruff circled wide, wanting to come up behind the Sioux. His eyes were on the three mounted men, his ears alert to the continuing gunfire racketing up the dark slopes, and so he nearly walked into the other warrior before he saw him.

The brave was sitting on the ground, wrapping a bandage around the calf of his leg. He came to his feet, mouth dropping open, and Ruff lunged. He had to take him quickly and silently, before the warning yell could emerge from that drooping mouth.

Even as Ruff flung himself through the air he was reaching for his belted Bowie. The knife came easily to hand, and he hit the Indian hard, clamping a hand across his mouth even as his knife thrust upward, driving deeply into the belly of the Sioux, under the V formed by the joining ribs. The knife found heart muscle, and the Indian, thrashing violently beneath Ruff's iron grip, died.

Shaken, Ruff recovered his Spencer and continued through the darkness, more cautiously now. The ground was broken, and twice he went down, once jolting a knee hard enough to leave that leg temporarily paralyzed.

Staggering on, he was finally behind the three warriors. Casually they joked with one another, reloaded their rifles, and fired into the ring of wagons. They were thoroughly enjoying themselves.

Ruff had been right about one thing—these were young men, perhaps too young to ride with the great war bands of Ta-Shaka. Their inexperience would risk the safety of the elite fighting force. Which showed that Ta-Shaka himself was no fool. The inexperience of these young Sioux was going to cost them.

Ruff whistled softly, and he saw three heads come around. Whispered conference followed. One brave shrugged, looked toward the low brush where Ruff was lying, his rifle at the ready. A second quick conference, and the warrior to the right started forward. Ruff held his fire, knowing he would have to take them all in the first barrage, get the hell away from the scene of the firefight, and circle back toward the wagons without being seen by the rest of the scattered Sioux.

He whistled again and settled in behind the sights, the curved trigger of his Spencer .56 cool under his taut index finger. The investigating warrior walked his pale pony forward. He was within fifty feet when Ruff triggered off the big Spencer and the Sioux was blasted from the horse's back, his arms outflung, a gaping hole carved by the huge .56 caliber bullet torn in his chest.

Ruff levered in a fresh cartridge and had fired at the man on his left before the Sioux had registered exactly what was happening. Most of his head was blown off, and even as the last remaining Sioux tried to absorb the reality of this, tried to knee his pony into motion, Ruff's big Spencer barked again and the warrior, his face blank, his eyes rolled back to show only white, toppled from the back of his horse. The horse danced away, eyes wide with fright, and Ruff came forward, thumbing three fresh cartridges into the Spencer.

He snatched up the reins to the lone Indian pony which hadn't gone galloping off across the hills while Ruff was spraying death at the Sioux, and walking behind it he moved eastward, working his way toward the cluster of snipers visible on a low bluff there.

There was a spurt of activity from nearer the wagon train, and as Ruff watched, a dozen Sioux charged the camp on foot. The settlers were up to it this time, however, and a barrage of withering fire drove the warriors back into the night. Ruff saw three of them left behind on the shadowed plains.

He moved on, not wanting to fire on the Sioux below and give his position away. Not yet. Distant thunder rumbled, and Ruff smiled, looking skyward minutes later as the first of the rain began to fall, drawing an iron curtain around him, screening his movements.

There were now two bodies of Sioux warriors Ruff knew about. Those ahead of him—he made their number to be about four—and those who had attacked the wagon train frontally and were now retreating. These were still being pursued by rifle fire, although Justice wondered how anyone could see to hit anything just now.

The rain was increasing, and with it came the heavy winds of previous days. Ruff tightened his grip on the Indian pony's bridle, only a loosely knotted loop of rope, and continued toward the nest of young Sioux ahead of him.

He thought he still had a good five hundred yards to go, but either he had become lost in the rain or, more likely, the Sioux themselves were moving. They were suddenly in front of him, and for a brief, indecisive moment the Sioux eyed the buckskin-clad figure leading the painted Indian horse through the veil of rain.

It was a moment too long. Ruff slapped the horse hard on the flank and it leaped forward, trampling two of the Sioux as Ruff went to a knee and levered three rounds through the Spencer, adding a hail of deadly lead to the falling rain.

A man screamed, his voice rising to meet the thundering storm before it was drowned out by the crack and flash of thunder and lightning.

An arrow sailed past Ruff's head and a flying, spinning hunk of red-hot lead tore at the calf of his leg. He threw himself to one side, losing his Spencer in the process. But he had palmed his Colt, its familiar weight reassuring, savage in his grip.

He thumbed the hammer back four times in succession and let those who were coming in have it. One crumpled like an unstrung marionette and went down, head thrown back, chest crimson. The second made it a near thing.

He leaped at Ruff, knife flashing, and Ruff, triggering off again, watched the rose of flame explode from the blue-black muzzle of the Colt, watched the man's head exploded as the 200-grain lead bullet split skull and tissue like a ripe melon.

The Indian landed sprawled across Ruff's chest, his warm blood leaking onto Ruff. Ruff lay still for a long minute, feeling the cold rain wash the blood away, feeling the weight of the Sioux's body, the hot pain in his lower leg.

Then, shoving the Indian aside, he rose to a sitting position and, Colt still in hand, tested his calf gingerly. He couldn't see a damn thing. All he knew was that it hurt like hell but the bone wasn't broken. He placed his palm on the wound, and it came away slick with warm blood.

Muttering a curse, Ruff produced a scarf from his pocket and tied it on tightly. Then he got to his feet, feeling only a little dizzy—it couldn't be bleeding much, he thought. Oddly the leg felt better as he stood and moved than it had sitting still in the downpouring rain. Perhaps that was because he already had his mind working on other problems.

Were there still more Sioux, or would they withdraw? It seemed to him that these four he had encountered had been moving off, but that may have been just to regroup with the rest of their war party. There was no telling, and so he moved with caution through the steadily falling rain, keeping his rifle at waist level, his thumb on the hammer.

The wagons sat in a dark, silent circle below him. Ruff eased to the edge of a small bluff and watched patiently. After half an hour the rain stopped again and the moon shook itself loose from the surrounding clouds to bleed pale light across the plains.

Nothing.

He saw no Sioux, heard no movement, no reports of weapons. It was as still and silent as if there had been no battle. He noticed the dead and wounded Sioux that he had spotted earlier had been dragged away under cover of the rain storm.

Now he saw a shadowy movement within the camp perimeter, and then another. They were moving about now, figuring the attack was over. Ruff hoped it was. But the menace was hardly gone, blown away like the storm clouds. Ta-Shaka was still out there. Ta-Shaka, who had sworn that no white man would live within sight of the sacred Black Hills. Ta-Shaka and his thousand battle-hardened warriors against this handful of arrogant interlopers.

Ruff limped toward the camp, coming carefully forward, calling out to avoid being shot by an overeager settler. His leg had begun to tighten up, and he was shivering with the cold by the time he made the circle of wagons, squeezed through the crates which formed a hastily thrown-up barricade, and was greeted.

"Where in hell have you been?" Buffalo Head demanded.

"Hiding out, most likely," a second man scoffed.

"First sign of trouble and our famous plainsman takes off," a third settler remarked.

They were all puffed up with victory, and Ruff let them make their comments. His leg left him very little enthusiasm for pushing someone's face in. He stumped past a shirtsleeved Caleb Waters. The would-be sutler turned his head away deliberately.

"How many hit?" Ruff asked.

"I don't see what the hell you care!"

"How many?" Ruff demanded. He came up chest to chest with Waters, and the man read the cold menace in Ruff's eyes.

"Four. Two men, one woman. Woman's pretty badly hit."

"You said four."

"The Indian . . ." Waters blinked. "Didn't you know? The Indian took a bullet in the first charge. Hey, Justice, where are you going?"

Ruff didn't answer. He was already halfway across the camp, moving toward the temporary hospital. Four beds had been made up on the ground, and there a sodbuster woman was working over the wounded while a man with a rifle in the crook of his arm held a lantern for her.

The nurse was working on a woman in a once-blue dress. Even from there Ruff could see the woman was in bad shape. It was her arm and chest. Blood, unchecked despite tourniquets, stained the ground around her.

Reggie was in even worse shape. No one was trying to help him—there was nothing more to be done. He lay in the shadow of a wagon, the firelight from a torch lighting only one half of his shattered face.

Ruff crouched down beside him, and Reggie looked up with one glittering, fevered eye. "You'll make it, Reggie."

Reggie knew otherwise. One side of his skull was torn open, and his chest rose and fell convulsively. Blood darkened his features. His hand trembled uncontrollably. Ruff found a cloth and a bucket of water beside Reggie, and he dipped the rag in water, wrung it out, folded it, and placed it on Reggie's burning forehead.

"Sorry about this, Reggie."

The trembling hand reached out and touched Ruff's wrist. " 'S all right, old boy . . . wasn't . . ."

Reggie tried to catch his breath and wasn't able to. He rolled his head toward Ruff, and Justice saw Reggie's left eye protruding unnaturally from a misshapen skull. The eye already seemed dead.

"Don't talk."

"Wasn't . . ." The grip of Reggie's hand was amazingly strong. "Wasn't damned Sioux . . ." He panted.

"It wasn't the Sioux? Who was it? Who got you, Reggie?"

The head rolled from side to side. He didn't know, apparently.

"Say, old boy . . . see that my remains are taken home, will you?" Reggie asked with sudden clarity. "See that these bones are taken home."

"Sure." Ruff attempted a smile. "I'll see to that."

Reggie's face seemed to relax at that. The single eye was peering up at him. The life seemed to be slowly seeping out of the Arik.

"Dammit!" Reggie shouted, but behind the shout there was more than pain. A sort of excitement seemed to surge through him. "I've got it now!"

"Got what, old man?" Ruff asked.

"All of it . . . combs, you know. *Combs.*"

"What?" Ruff shook his head. Reggie's hand had dropped away now. "What's that, Reggie?"

Now he wanted him to talk, to answer him, to smile, to call him old man, old sport, old boy, in that mock-British accent, to tell him all about riding to the hounds, about the lovely Elena Chalmers and his passion for her.

But he would never speak of any of it again. He lay there, eye gleaming coldly. Dead. Ruff covered the body and rose, his mouth tight. Just then the terrible scream of a suffering woman rode through the night on wings of panic and was silenced. Another one would not make it.

Ruff glanced that way and saw them covering the face of the wounded settler woman. Spotting Caleb Waters, he strode toward him, rifle in hand.

"Is there anyone named Combs or Coombs with this train, Waters?"

"What? You, is it, Justice? Get out of my sight."

"Damn you!" Ruff grabbed a handful of shirtfront and shook the wagon-train leader so violently that his head snapped back and forth. "I asked you a question,

Waters." His voice was a low, menacing hiss that demanded an answer.

"No . . . I mean, no." He gasped, "Why?"

"Because it wasn't the Indians that got Reggie. He told me that before he died."

"He's dead, I'm—"

"Yes, I'll bet you are." Ruff threw the man away from him. "Dammit, Waters—there's some rotten business going on here. Who the hell was Averill Curtis? You know who he was, a damned outlaw. The man just attempted to rob the bank in Bismarck a few days ago. They killed Tom Dukes, the marshal. Why was he guiding this train?"

"I really couldn't . . ." Waters stammered.

"He was murdered, in case you've forgotten in the excitement. Murdered by your daughter, perhaps conspiring with her husband. Why? He attacked her? That won't wash—your daughter likely would have welcomed it."

Waters started to sputter at that, but Ruff cut him off. "Someone killed Reggie. Now who in hell would do that? Why? Waters, something stinks in this setup, and either you know about it and you're behind it, or you should damn well be making an effort to find out what it is."

"With the Sioux, with . . . !" Waters regained himself enough to stir up genuine anger.

"The Sioux, likely, will come up on us and kill every living thing with this train. But at least you'll see them coming, and you'll know exactly who you've got to blame for riding into this mess."

"Me." Waters hung his head. His fingers played nervously across his forehead. "I know it. Dammit, I know it! It's my fault, every bit of it. I should have listened to you, Justice. I guess I knew you were right all along. But I couldn't bear to lose that money, can you understand that? If you can't sympathize, can't you at least understand?"

Ruff nodded, his mouth still tight with distaste.

Waters licked his lips. "This is all my doing—but about the rest of it, God help me, I know nothing. My only concern now is with getting these people through to Grizzly, if it's still possible." He paused, looking very weary and beaten. "You are our only chance to do that, Justice. I know you've got other objectives, but can you turn your back on these people now? I got us into this, but I'm asking . . . begging you to help us get out of it."

Ruff couldn't reply to him. Not just then. Caleb Waters was slowly crumbling, his composure turning to the consistency of jelly. Whatever he had thought himself to be, he was discovering he was not. He was the man who had purchased death for these people. He was the man whose cupidity was responsible for the letting of blood. His daughter was a murderess, a savage if beautiful thing—it was slowly beginning to sink in, and the taste of it was bitter.

So was the taste in the mouth of Ruff Justice as he buried the man he had known as Reginald Darby-Smythe. He realized that he had never known his true name, the one his mother and father had given to him as they marveled at his arrival into this harsh and cold world.

Reggie was dead now. Buried. He had asked to have his bones buried at home. It wasn't possible—if he had meant England. Yet somehow Ruff thought that at the last Reggie had meant he wished to be buried here. Here where the long winds blew, where the buffalo wandered untrammeled across the broad plains, where life was raw and savage and clean.

"You're home, Reggie," he said over the grave as the wind drifted his long dark hair across his face.

Home; buried in the earth he had sprung from. Maybe he had not meant to be buried here, but there was no other choice. The question troubling Ruff just now was what had the man meant by "combs." A clue to his murderer? A ciphered message to the never forgotten Elena Chalmers, a plan to capture MacAdoo and Slaussen, a way to evade the Sioux . . . Christ! Who knew. Not Ruff. But it had been the word spoken with his last breath— that alone made it important.

He had let Reggie down, perhaps, burying him out here

with only the coyotes and the buzzards as witnesses. Could he ignore another plea, a last message? *Combs*.

A name, a woman's hairpiece, a search, a rooster's ornament—what? "What, Reggie?"

But there was no answer, and the grave, fresh, dark, and cold, lay silent and restless before him. Ruff stood there until sunrise colored the long plains, until red and deep-orange fire played across the clouds, until the first narrow filament of beaten gold strung itself out across the dark horizon. Then he turned and strode toward the circle of wagons, which still waited, stunned, confused, motionless in the dawn light.

There had been a ceremony for the dead woman, and around the fresh grave stood Caleb Waters, Abigail, Shaughnessy, a man with an anguished face, his arm in a sling, Buffalo Head, and the man named Carl.

Ruff slipped up beside Waters as the sun shone on the dewy grass, lighting it with a thousand jewels of red and yellow, blue and green.

"Let's move this train out," Ruff said. "Hitch those oxen, Waters. We've got a hundred miles and a thousand Sioux to go."

10

THE SUN WAS still low, warm on Ruff's back, when he led the wagon train out, westward, toward Grizzly. He had considered turning east, returning to Bismarck, but after scouting a mile out he rejected that idea—they were cut off. The plains were swarming with Sioux and Cheyenne, and he had seen a temporary camp due east which held fifty men at the minimum.

So it was Grizzly or nothing. Ruff could only lead them off the main road and try to elude the watching Sioux by traveling a half-circle route slightly north of the flat trail. The going was slower, and he had no real confidence that this plan would do anything to fool the Indians. It was impossible that a wagon train could pass unseen.

Yet they saw no hostiles for mile after mile. Sun-silvered high clouds were banked against the pale-blue skies. The earth beneath the wagon wheels was sodden, sticky, dark. The long grass was green, bending in the northern breeze. At noon they saw a large buffalo herd, patiently grazing its way southward. They waited nearly an hour for the massive herd to pass.

"Looks like you were wrong," Buffalo Head said. His name, as it turned out, was Jake Thurgood, a farmer who had gone bust in Minnesota and had been evicted from his homestead. He had no choice but to move to new land in the Dakota Territory. Thurgood, massive and slow as

101

he seemed, was quick-witted, and if not exactly friendly, he was at least clear-eyed and steady. Ruff had taken him as his second in command.

"Wrong?" Ruff's head turned toward Thurgood. "You mean about the Sioux? No. You saw the camp this morning."

"That was east of here."

"And they're south of here. And north, probably. Look, Thurgood, I know Caleb Waters thinks I've got reasons for wanting this expedition to fail, probably he's told you that— Hold those oxen!" An untended team had started to creep forward to join the buffalo with the instincts of herding animals. Ruff saw the sodbuster jump for his team. He continued, "I'm not opposed to you people doing whatever the hell you like. Except that I'd hate to see you murdered. I've seen a sight too much of bloodshed on these plains."

"All right," Thurgood said softly. "I believe you. Don't see why I shouldn't. Tell me this—is someone else trying to keep us from getting to Grizzly?"

"What do you mean?" Ruff asked. His gray shifted its feet and shook its head, causing its white mane to swirl around its neck like white mist.

"Just this—our scout was killed. Why? No one knows. The woman's sticking to her story, though no one believes it anymore. They'll play hell proving it was otherwise."

"You figure Curtis—or Grange, as I knew him—was killed to keep you from reaching Grizzly?"

"It's crossed my mind."

"I can't swallow it. He wasn't much of a scout; his game was bank robbery."

"We know that now—we didn't then. My thinking is that someone killed him *believing* without Averill Curtis we'd never reach Grizzly."

Ruff was thoughtful for a moment. That hadn't occurred to him, and he tended to discount it out of hand, but who knew what was going on here? It was a damned mess . . . and all the time Slaussen and MacAdoo were getting farther away.

The buffalo had cleared the wagon train, and Ruff lifted a hand, starting them forward again. He gave Thurgood a landmark to point for, a low, crumbling bluff which appeared only as a raised eyebrow on the horizon, but which was really, as Ruff knew, five hundred feet of rock and earth shaped like a ship's prow—hence its name, Schooner Bluff.

Ruff pulled away from the wagons, catching a last dubious glance from Thurgood. What was going through the big man's head? Maybe he thought Ruff was pulling out for good.

The air was cold and clean, and the grass trembled in the wind as if the entire earth shuddered. The clouds whipped past rapidly, and the sun, shining between gaps in the cloud cover, formed quick-running sunspots which raced across the prairie ahead of Ruff's gray.

The wind turned back the hatbrim of his black hat, and his hair fluttered out behind him. He surveyed the immense, raw land to the south and west, searching for Sioux, but also indulging his eyes, his soul. The land seemed endless, and it was revitalizing, bracing. Here he was alive, only here.

Justice had spent time with his friend Bill Cody in Europe, and in New York and San Francisco. Bill, cleverer by far than some thought, was selling his own share of the Western dream to hungry civilized man.

They had lived well, dressed fancy, met the proud aristocrats, the financiers . . . and their women. But the city stifled the soul; a man became blind and poor and desperate. Not here! Not out here!

Here a man could almost understand his life, almost understand God. Except that God seemed more properly the Great Manitou—this was an Indian's land, and the god was his, the land his creation.

Ruff came across the tracks in a shallow coulee. He sat the gray horse for a long while, his eyes sweeping the horizons, before he swung down, rifle in hand, and squatted, assuring himself of what he already knew—the three horses were those of MacAdoo's gang.

He recognized the slight toe-in of the big horse, the chip in the shoe of another, the tendency of the third to drag its right front.

Straightening up, Ruff looked westward.

Grizzly. By God, they were riding toward Grizzly, or near it!

Puzzled, he stepped into leather again. *Comb. Averill Curtis. Grizzly. Abigail. Waters. Sioux.* It wouldn't come clear. He had all the pieces, or maybe all but one—the central piece, the keystone. None of this added up, and Ruff felt blind, stupid, angry.

Grizzly was or wasn't deserted. Slaussen and MacAdoo were or weren't going there to meet or not meet Grange, who had been murdered by Abigail Waters with or without reason.

He thumped his fist against his head, but it wouldn't come clear. It didn't matter. Just then none of it mattered. All that did matter was that MacAdoo and Slaussen were ahead of him—and they were his meat.

The MacAdoo gang could have been going anywhere, of course, but why not Grizzly? Especially if it was deserted or nearly so? Ruff knew it then. Knew that Grizzly was MacAdoo's objective.

His impulse was to get on the trail of the MacAdoo gang and stick there. Yet nothing had changed in the past few minutes—he still had an obligation to the people in the Waters caravan. An obligation he had not asked for, had not wanted, but which was nevertheless a real obligation.

His eyes lifting wistfully toward the distant town of Grizzly, Ruff turned back toward the wagon train.

His rage, he had noticed, was dying. The heated emotions were cooling. None of that would do Slaussen or MacAdoo any good. They would die. They had crossed the line and entered the dark hemisphere of the beasts—those who crept through the night and preyed on the weak, extinguishing life as if it were nothing. Such as these Ruff would not suffer to walk the same clean earth with him.

Schooner Bluff loomed black and massive against the darkening skies as Ruff walked the big gray horse down a shallow gully toward the wagon train. Thurgood still rode at the point, his face as impassive as ever. Caleb Waters, appearing smaller, shrunken, sat the seat of his lumbering wagon, his eyes flitting past Ruff Justice as the tall man in buckskins rode in.

Behind him the Shaughnessy wagon rolled. Abigail sat subdued, but apparently not defeated, judging by the spark in her dark eyes, beside the stolid bulk of her husband. Brent Shaughnessy did appear defeated. His face, still colored from the fight with Justice, appeared doughy and slack. Both deliberately averted their eyes as Ruff rode past.

"How far?" Thurgood asked as Justice drew abreast.

Ruff looked toward Schooner Bluff and guessed: twenty miles.

"That means tonight!" Thurgood said, having difficulty keeping the exultation out of his voice.

"Jake," Ruff said soberly, "I know what you're thinking, what you're hoping for. Grizzly is a refuge to you. Once there you'll be surrounded by hundreds of armed townspeople—hardly the sort of target Ta-Shaka or any other hostile likes. I don't think it's going to be that way. I'm afraid you and your people won't be any safer there than you are out here."

"No. Well, I don't believe it, Justice. Have you been there?" At Ruff's negative shake of the head, Jake Thurgood went on, "I'll continue to believe what Curtis told us. I know, I know, he was no scout at all. But from watching the man it was plain enough to me that he's been over this country before. I can't see why he'd lie about there being folks in Grizzly."

"No? Simply to get you there, Thurgood. Tell me, did Averill Curtis have anything to do with helping Waters to make up his mind in the first place—before you had even left Bismarck, that is?"

Thurgood scratched his whiskered throat. "Yes, I guess you could say he did. He assured Mr. Waters that Grizzly was flourishing. But I don't get it, Justice. What you're saying is that Curtis was lying all along. Why would he do that?"

"I don't know for sure, but I've got an idea. I suppose we won't know until we get to Grizzly, will we? One piece of advice I do have to give you, Thurgood—ride loose, man. There's more trouble out here just now than you've imagined. And all of it isn't wearing paint and feathers."

The sun faded behind the silvery clouds before settling toward the dark line of the horizon and emitting a last desperate flush of crimson. Ruff Justice wore his buffalo coat now, the collar turned up against the blasts of wind. He was a quarter of a mile ahead of the wagon train when he finally saw Grizzly, and he sat the low knoll, looking down into the valley at the darkened town.

Looking back, he saw Jake Thurgood approaching, dwarfing the stunted pony he rode. Behind Jake was the wagon train, silent but for the screeching of ungreased wheels. Ruff removed his hat, waved it toward Thurgood, and wiped back his long hair before replacing the hat.

"Grizzly?" Thurgood's voice was so enthusiastic that Ruff hated to see the crestfallen expression which followed as he got a good long look at the town of Grizzly, Dakota Territory.

"Empty," Thurgood said numbly. "Looks like you were right all along."

"It doesn't give me any satisfaction," Ruff told him. He looked across his shoulder to see the Waters's wagon drawing toward them. Caleb Waters's face was puzzled, expectant, pale.

"Is it . . . ?" he asked, and then he saw it too. He breathed a slow, throttled curse. "Deserted!" He looked to Justice for help. "What now, Justice? What now?"

"We'll go on in. There's not much other choice, is there?"

"No." Waters looked again at the dark, silent town. "No, there isn't much other choice."

"Why?" Thurgood said heavily. "Why did Curtis lie to us? Why did he say the town was inhabited?"

"I'll tell you what I think," Ruff answered. "It's time that you knew what you're up against. Curtis, or Grange, ran with an outlaw band. A few days ago they tried to rob the bank in Bismarck. It didn't work, but even if it had, the gang, under a man named Amos MacAdoo, had a problem. They had to run, and the only place to run with any hope of security was out onto the plains." Ruff paused and looked at the three men—Brent Shaughnessy had joined them.

"MacAdoo doesn't appear to be a fool. He was planning ahead, win or lose on the bank job. Now, to hole up out here he needed privacy and he needed one other thing—supplies enough to wait out Ta-Shaka. Well . . ." Ruff nodded toward Grizzly. "He's got his privacy. And"—he nodded toward the wagons—"it looks as if he's got his supplies."

"Are you saying that Curtis . . . Grange was planted on us to guide this wagon train through to Grizzly?" Waters wanted to know.

"That's exactly what I'm saying. It was no secret that you were hanging around Bismarck looking for a guide, no secret that you had plenty of valuable goods—food, ammunition, blankets, everything MacAdoo and his men would need. What they didn't need they intended to sell off when and if the army pushed Ta-Shaka back into Canada."

"But *we* . . ."

"You, Mr. Waters, were going to be killed. Every last one of you, women and children included. Nothing to it—Ta-Shaka and his warriors would take the blame. It wouldn't take much work to make it look like the Sioux's doing."

"In that case . . ." Waters looked toward the empty town. "They are down there now."

"That's the way my figuring goes," Ruff agreed. "With an ambush set up."

"This is preposterous!" Brent Shaughnessy spat. "How do we know they're down there at all? You've never wanted us to reach Grizzly."

"No, for obvious reasons. But here we find ourselves. Tell me, Shaughnessy, was it you, your wife, or the both of you who threw in with the MacAdoo gang in planning this?"

"Why, you son of a bitch," Brent Shaughnessy said slowly, and for a moment the old anger flared up in his eyes.

Caleb Waters started to object, but Ruff held up a hand. "It had to be that way. Who was it who encouraged Caleb here to come ahead? Both of you? What was your percentage going to be, Shaughnessy? Half? Or only a bullet in the head? Sure, that's why Curtis was killed—crime of passion!" Ruff laughed harshly. "It was plain murder, cutting out another partner."

"I don't have to take this, Justice," Shaughnessy sputtered.

"No," he said, shaking his head. "No, you don't, but you're going to have to take what's coming next."

Ruff's level gaze met Shaughnessy's, and the big man, with an explosive expulsion of breath, spun on his heel and stalked away.

"Why the hell can't you forget all of these grudges, Justice?" Waters asked. His voice was nearly breaking. Sad eyes fixed themselves on Ruff.

"Why?" Ruff asked tonelessly.

"Of course, you had a fight with Brent. Forget it. I made certain remarks. Can't we forget all of this and work together?"

"We could," Ruff said. "If I could forget one thing."

"What's that?"

"One of you killed Reggie. Cold-bloodedly murdered the man. Was it you, Waters?"

Caleb Waters nearly staggered. He had to lean against his lead oxen for support. "Are you . . . why no! No, dammit, and I won't believe Brent Shaughnessy did it either. Or . . ." He swallowed hard.

"Or Abigail? She's already shown she has the capacity, Waters."

"She had no choice in that situation," Waters said, gathering himself.

"No?" Ruff frowned. "Maybe she found herself in another situation where she 'had no choice.' "

"You are . . ." Whatever Waters thought Ruff was, Justice was never to learn. The old man's voice fell away into a shaky grumble. The finger leveled at him continued to accuse, indefinitely. Ruff lifted his eyes.

Jake Thurgood was watching him, his sidelong gaze not unfriendly, yet without warmth. "What do you think?" Thurgood asked, nodding at the dark, squat town before them.

"I think we'd best go in slow and easy," Ruff answered. "They're killers, Thurgood, and they want what we've got."

Thurgood nodded his understanding. They were in a situation now where the supplies themselves might mean life or death to them. The wagon train would have to hole up in Grizzly, fortify the town as well as possible, and hope to withstand Ta-Shaka. But without food and supplies they wouldn't make it long—no one was going to go out hunting for meat.

"How do you want to do it, Justice?"

"Let it get full dark." Ruff squatted on his heels. "I'll swing around to the far side of town and come up that side street." Ruff lifted a finger, indicating the street he meant. "The rest of you come in easy, fan out, and take it building by building. Keep the wagon train back until we've cleaned them out. Unless you can think of another way?" He lifted an eyebrow, and Jake Thurgood had to wag his head.

"No. I'll pass the word along."

"Jake?" Ruff stood and walked to his gray. "Do me a favor—keep Waters and Shaughnessy in front of you."

"You still think they're mixed up in this?"

"Somebody is. I think, yes, somebody is working with the MacAdoo gang. If I'm wrong, well, I don't think either of them would mind shooting me on general principles if he gets a chance."

Thurgood shrugged massively, his face unconvinced. Then he ambled off to inform the rest of his men. Ruff tightened his cinch and walked the big gray down into the darkened valley, glancing over his shoulder at the bulk of Schooner Bluff, at the hesitant silver moon peering through a break in the clouds.

There was a stream running past at the edge of town—the city water supply, and just now it was swift and cold. Ruff forded it, the water going to his horse's knees, and he circled wide through the heavy sagebrush and nopal cactus.

He watched the town for lights, expecting to see none. MacAdoo had proved he was no fool. Mad he might be, but he was hardly stupid. They would have had someone posted to watch for the wagon train. Now they would be forted up, waiting, weapons cocked.

Ruff was behind the town, the moon shining faintly on him through the bulk of the dark oaks which towered overhead. The stream glinted silver in the moonlight. The town was deathly silent.

He could see nothing of the wagon train, hear nothing of the men who now should be approaching the town, beginning the slow search.

There could be but one result of that search. There would be fighting and death. Justice regretted it, regretted bringing these people into this, but they had been forewarned.

His mind now shifted to still darker thoughts—thoughts of vengeance, cold, slow vengeance, for he was out there somewhere, the man who had killed Louise and made the days all seem less bright, taking her laughing eyes, her smile from the world.

"You haven't gotten away with a damn thing, Slaussen," Ruff whispered to the night. "I only hope you don't go and get yourself killed before I can do it."

He glanced once again at the moon, which was now going dark as the rolling clouds swept across the sky once again. Then, kneeing the big gray, he started forward toward the dark, silent town; a silent, hunting man, an

110

avenging spirit, a dark angel riding. And ahead lay the savagery of battle. Ahead lay the pursued, the condemned, and Ruff was carrying the means of retribution, caliber .44–40.

11

THE INTERIOR OF the livery barn was musty, dark, and silent. Ruff opened the outer door and then waited, crouching low. When there was no gunfire he slipped quickly inside, staying low to avoid any bullets. But the barn remained silent.

He walked his gray forward, slipped the saddle and bit, and left it there to munch on alfalfa hay which was still fresh and sweet. Returning to the doorway, he paused a moment, looking down the side street. It had a name. A plank was tacked to a pole on the corner, but from there Ruff could not read the sign.

He moved out into the street, pistol cocked and elevated, the barrel next to his ear. He heard nothing from the far side of town, but then he shouldn't have been able to if Thurgood's men were doing their job properly.

Ruff crossed the street and pressed himself against the side of the building—a dressmaker's shop. He glanced in the dark, quartered window, seeing nothing but an undraped tailor's dummy.

Ruff drew away. The town was enough to disturb a man. Ruff had been in true ghost towns before, but never in a town like Grizzly where it seemed people might walk out of the silent saloon at any moment, where nothing was altered, broken, cobwebbed, dusty. The shelves in the stores had been emptied, but outside of that there was no indication that the town was not thriving, that the inhabitants weren't merely sleeping.

But they weren't. The inhabitants had run, run from the plague of warfare and blood, run from Ta-Shaka's path. Ruff tested the side door of the dressmaker's shop, found it locked, and applied his shoulder twice.

The lock wasn't much, and the door popped open. Ruff, stepping inside, went to the side, and when there was no barrage of bullets, searched slowly and carefully, creeping through the empty storeroom, the dressing cubicles.

Empty.

A packrat scrabbled across the floor and vanished into an unseen den, but there was nothing else, no one. From across town no shots rang out, although by now Thurgood and his men had to be making an intensive search of every building up and down Grizzly's short main street.

The next shop was a milliner's, and Ruff found only the same mocking emptiness. Now, emerging, he could hear Thurgood and his men. Someone laughed out loud, and Ruff frowned. It was hardly the time or place you'd expect laughter. Something was up.

Ruff walked out onto the street, and now from uptown he saw the glare of torchlight. Wagons were rolling up the main street of Grizzly, and the saloons, and the hotel were lighted with lanternlight.

Jake Thurgood, hands on hips, rifle in hand, stood directly in the middle of the street, looking around slowly, his buffalo head turning slowly, heavily. His small dark eyes fixed on Ruff Justice.

"What in the hell's going on?" Ruff demanded. "This is the way you quietly search a town?"

"Been searched!" the man named Carl jeered. He had found a bottle of whiskey somewhere and was now at it.

"What's he talking about?" Ruff demanded.

"We've been up one side of the street and down the other, Justice," Thurgood answered. "The results—absolutely nothing. There's nobody hiding in this town, no snipers, killers, Sioux or Cheyenne. Nobody," he said with emphasis.

"Impossible," Ruff said quietly.

"Is it?" The speaker was Caleb Waters. Behind and to his left stood Abigail Shaughnessy, her eyes as mocking as ever. From the saloon the sound of shattering glass echoed.

"What did you see, Justice?" Brent Shaughnessy demanded. He had appeared next to his wife, rifle in his thick hands. "There's no one here. You keep saying there's Sioux all around us. Well, we saw a few dozen, no more. You say this gang of outlaws is holed up in Grizzly—well, where in hell are they?"

That was a good question, and Ruff had no answer for the man. Not now.

He had seen the tracks heading toward Grizzly, and assumed that the town was their target. The rest of the plan as he had guessed it followed logically. Now, standing in the middle of the torchlit street, he was not so sure that he had drawn the right conclusions from the evidence he had seen.

"Well?" Caleb Waters again.

"I'm going to turn in," Ruff said quietly. "If I were you, I'd post a guard on the rooftops."

With that he turned and walked away, ignoring the laughter of several of the bystanders. He cared nothing for their mockery; all that mattered was that Slaussen and MacAdoo were not here. Where then? Dammit, where?

These people had their wish. They had made it to Grizzly. Let them face the Sioux and the hard land by themselves to the best of their ability. That was what they would have had to do anyway.

Ruff was washing his hands of them—of Abigail and Shaughnessy, of Caleb Waters. Well, maybe not completely. One of them, dammit, had killed Reggie. He knew that much. "Not Sioux," Reggie had said. But now, as Ruff settled down in the stable, making a bed of straw and his blankets, he wondered—did Reggie's words mean that it had been someone from the wagon train? "Not Sioux . . . Combs."

Someone named Combs? Something which sounded like "combs"? Reggie's voice had been weak by then.

Damn. There were no answers. Ruff rolled up in his blanket, his Colt in his hand, his horse standing near at hand. The night drifted past, whispering no answers. At midnight it began to rain again.

"Justice!"

Ruff sat up, his thumb on the hammer of the big single-action Colt. He pawed at his eyes, wiping away the sleep, the fatigue. He recognized the voice as Thurgood's, saw that the man was alone, that his rifle was not aimed his way, and sat up.

The door behind Thurgood was open and the rain pelted down. "What is it?" he asked wearily.

"Waters . . . Caleb Waters," Thurgood said dully. "He's missing."

"Missing," Ruff repeated slowly. "What in hell do you want me to do about it, Jake? He's missing. Go find him. Look in the saloons. The boys were having a good time in there last time I looked." And they had the place lighted up like sunrise, an invitation to Ta-Shaka and his renegades. Ruff had been tempted to pull out in the middle of the night. Only the weariness which slowed his flow of blood, made his feet feel like lead, dulled his wits had kept him in Grizzly this long.

"You don't understand," Jake Thurgood said, approaching Ruff to crouch down and spread his hands pleadingly. "We've looked everywhere. Thing is . . . he was in the hotel, in a room with no windows. Locked in and sleeping. After midnight we heard some kind of sound. A crackle, like. A creak. We called at the door, but no one answered. His daughter had a proper fit and demanded we break the door down. Well, we did.

"He wasn't there, Justice. A locked room with no way out, and he wasn't there!"

Ruff was pulling his boots on, his clouded mind struggling to free itself from the cobwebs.

115

"You searched everywhere?"

"Everywhere," Thurgood said excitedly. "Well, we were worried, damned worried. But not so worried as we got an hour or so later when it . . ."

"When what?" Ruff came to his feet, strapping on his gunbelt.

"All right—she's missing too. Abigail Shaughnessy. She was there, I mean in the hotel, outside her father's room, and then . . . she was gone."

"Wait a minute—they're *both* gone? And you don't know how or where?"

"That's about it."

"Damn," Ruff said softly.

"What do you think?"

Ruff had planted his hat on his head. Now, snatching up his Spencer repeater, he turned to look at Thurgood. "You know what I think, Jake."

"MacAdoo?" Jake's heavy eyebrows drew together.

"Somehow, yes. Somehow he's involved, for whatever reason." He nodded his head toward the open stable door. "Let's go see if we can find out just why."

They plodded up the main street, sticking to the awnings over the boardwalk when they could. The rain hurled itself angrily against the earth. Lightning seemed to crumble the sky; the thunder was a cannon barrage, the wind a lashing howl.

"Here we are."

Ruff followed Thurgood into the hotel, seeing the settlers sleeping on the lobby floor. Blank eyes looked up at him. In the corner at the entrance to a narrow, dark corridor, three men with rifles in hand stood staring soberly at Ruff and Thurgood.

"Anything?" Jake asked as they approached the men.

"No." It was Carl who answered, sparing a moment to smirk at Justice. The others didn't seem so amused by events. People were disappearing and they had no way of knowing who might be next.

"Let's have a look," Ruff said.

"There's nothing to see," Carl objected. Carl Hinton, a

116

dark-eyed, thin-haired man with long, pale hands, had been a banker, a rancher, a silversmith, a wainwright, a court secretary, and a buffalo hunter in turn. He had failed spectacularly at each and every occupation. That had never dampened his confidence, his inexplicable ego.

His eyes met those of Ruff Justice now, perhaps for the first time. That is, he had spoken to Ruff, looked at him, but he had never really *seen* the man. Now he did, and what he saw was wire and leather, iron and cold blue eyes, competence beyond anything Hinton in his various muddled careers had dreamed of. He backed away, the smile clinging to his lips like a comic and bizarre remnant of a long-dead clown's expression.

"This way," Thurgood said.

He led off down the corridor, his bootheels clicking on the uncarpeted floor. The scent of powder and of whiskey lingered in the hallway from long-ago guests, shadows of happier nights.

Ruff heard the clomping of heavy feet behind him, and turning his head, he saw Brent Shaughnessy, looking weary and drawn, following them. Justice halted.

"Get that man away from me," he said.

"Who? Shaughnessy?"

"Who do you think? Yes, Shaughnessy. I won't have him on my heels. I don't like him, I don't trust him, I don't want him near me."

"It's my wife that's missing," Shaughnessy shouted.

"You should have kept an eye on her—you must be used to doing that anyway."

Shaughnessy started forward, and Ruff shot a glance at Thurgood, who, reading the expression properly, indicated that Brent Shaughnessy should be restrained. All they needed now was another brawl.

Shaughnessy was escorted back to the lobby. Thurgood went to the next door, the third down the long low corridor, and palmed the handle. The door swung open on oiled hinges, and Ruff went into the room seeing at first glance that there were no windows, noticing the clothing laid out on the bed—Caleb Waters' clothing. A small .36

Remington pistol lay on the bed as well. There was no sign of a struggle.

"Just like I told you," Thurgood said. There was a hint of uneasiness in his gravelly voice.

"Uh-huh." Ruff moved around the room, nudging a carpet bag left on the floor with his toe.

"No way, you see," Thurgood said. Other faces peered in the doorway.

"There's obviously a way, Jake," Ruff said evenly. "If there was no way then Waters and Abigail would be here. Unless you're starting to believe in boogies."

Jake flushed, puffing up a little with a response swelling his throat. Ruff waved a hand at him, and he calmed slightly.

"Go on out," Ruff said. "I want to poke around."

"But . . ."

"Did you hear me?" He had his reasons, but he didn't want to explain it to Jake Thurgood.

"We'll be right outside," the big man said.

Ruff watched as they closed the door and went out. "All right," he said quietly after a minute, "I'm alone."

Nothing happened then, but he expected it would. Waters and Abigail had both vanished when they were alone. Meaning, perhaps, that whoever was responsible was possessed of limited strength and firepower. One person could be taken, a band of armed men no.

"I said I'm alone," he repeated, and at the sound of the grating squeak he turned his head to see the wall open up. A panel from ceiling to floor, joined where the planks of the wall met so that it was invisible to the casual eye, had swung open an inch or two. Ruff could see almost nothing in that opening, but he could plainly see the muzzle of a Winchester repeater.

The timorous voice said, "Put down that rifle and holster your Colt."

"No." Ruff didn't move. He looked at the small opening and waited.

"Didn't you hear me? I'll shoot."

"Will you? What's the point in it? I know where you

are, and if you shoot me, *they'll* know too." He nodded his head toward the closed hotel-room door.

There was a long thoughtful pause. Finally the voice said, "Well, come on over here then. Come slowly, easy now . . . that's right."

The panel opened another hair, and Ruff found there was room for him to squeeze inside the cold, hidden recess. It was dark and close behind the panel, but there was enough light for Ruff to get a glimpse of the woman before the section of wall closed tightly behind him.

For it was a woman he had been speaking to moments before, a woman who held the Winchester on him. But not Abigail Shaughnessy. Not at all; she was nothing like Abigail in appearance. Abigail was tall, full-breasted, sleek, polished, and haughty. This one was a mousy thing, very young, wearing a long drab coat and a man's flop hat. What Ruff could see of her eyes was alluring in its own way—huge, blue, long-lashed. Behind wings of colorless hair an uncertain face peered out. Small-mouthed, small-chinned, lips pursed in childish determination.

The barrel of the Winchester jabbed itself against Ruff's ribcage. "Jest don't think you've got me buffaloed," the voice, hardly hesitant now, warned.

He grinned in the darkness. He didn't know which of the two was the taller, the Winchester or the girl; but it didn't matter. It doesn't take much strength to pull a trigger.

"Where are they?" he asked.

"Your friends?" she replied, her voice sneering.

"The people you captured."

"Move on ahead," she said without answering him. "I'm walkin' right behind you, mister."

"Justice," he said as the girl shifted around behind him, placing the muzzle of that Winchester against his spine.

"What?"

"Ruffin T. Justice is my name, miss."

"Kind of a funny name, ain't it?"

"Could be—hadn't thought of it as such." Nor had a

lot of other people. It was a name which tended to make those familiar with the stories shiver a little.

Ruff, prodded along, felt his way down a narrow plank-floored corridor. It was dark as sin.

"Watch it now," she cautioned. "Floor changes."

She was right about that, although Ruff didn't expect it to change so abruptly and so dramatically. The planking fell away and Ruff felt his boot slip. The floor was native stone, slick and rough.

"What is this?" he asked.

No answer. The rifle prodded him again.

"What exactly is this about? Where are we going?"

No answer.

Ruff trudged on, finding that the corridor, though winding first left and then right, continued always to tend slightly downward. Already he would have estimated they were fifty feet beneath the ground level of Grizzly.

It was pitch-black now and Ruff had slowed to a crawl.

"What's holding you up?" the girl demanded.

"I can't see—what do you think would be holding me up?"

"No need to get testy," she answered.

Ruff fell silent. He waited until they had taken ten more steps, turning around a narrow corner. Then he dropped to the floor of the corridor and rolled back sharply. His body hit the girl's legs and she went down.

Ruff grappled for the Winchester, tearing it from her small hands before she could react. Then, straddling the girl, hands on her shoulders, Ruff said, "Now we can go on."

"Why you damned . . ." she sputtered and twisted, trying to free herself.

"Ruff Justice," he told her, preferring that name to the one she was about to spit out.

"Beatin' up on a woman!"

"A woman with a rifle in my back."

"And I trusted you!"

"I'll bet. Let's go on ahead, shall we? This time"—he

helped her to her feet—"you lead. I don't know the way, Miss Wildcat."

"Haynes! Virginia Haynes," she shouted. Ruff couldn't see the expression on the young woman's face; he could barely make her out in the darkness, which was nearly complete. But he didn't have to see her to imagine her genuine fury. She had spirit, this one, and he liked her for it.

"Move out," was all he said. "Hold it a minute." He stretched out a hand and took hold of her coat tail. "I wouldn't want you running off from me, Ginny."

"Virginia . . . !" she started to complain, but there wasn't much point in arguing with a man in this situation.

"Mind telling me what you're doing down here?" He paused; there was no answer, no sound at all but the muffled clicking of their boots as they moved deeper into the cavern. "Mind telling me why you took those people prisoner? Or are they prisoners?" No answer. "Mind telling me where we are, where we're going?" She seemed to mind each question, and Ruff, sighing, let it drop.

Still holding onto her coat, Ruff followed the girl down a long natural stone chute. He worked his way only by feel, and felt sure that if he lost hold of her coat he would have the devil's own time finding his way back out of here. Here? What was here? A deep maze of a cavern beneath Grizzly.

He could hear water running off to his left. A thin, trickling sound. Ground seep, likely from the week's rain.

Light. He saw the pale glow of light and halted abruptly, yanking back on the girl's coat. She tripped slightly, stumbling toward him, and her skull rapped Ruff's nose.

"Who's that?" he whispered.

"Thought you knew everything," she mocked.

"I feel like I don't know a damn thing," Ruff snapped. "What am I getting into here? I'd advise you to tell me—I don't like finding myself trapped. I tend to shoot whatever gets in my way—nearest things first."

"Oh," she laughed harshly, "you are a mean one. Kill

and cuss and threaten, Lord! Look—it's my Pa up ahead with your two friends. That's all."

"You sure?"

"That's what I said. I'm not going to say everything twice for you, Mr. Tuffin."

"Ruffin. Ruff Justice."

"Yes," she replied shortly. "Are you ready now? Come ahead."

Justice didn't know if he was ready or not, but he made himself as ready as possible. Clutching the girl's coat, his pistol free and ready in his right hand, he followed her toward the light, which was glaring, painful to the eyes in this black sinkhole.

They went around a second bend, up a narrow, water-slick chute, and then were there.

"Pa?"

At the sound of the girl's voice, the old man who had been holding his rifle on Waters and Abigail turned his white head toward the entrance to the small, lanternlit alcove.

"Virginia . . ." He muttered a curse, his eyes locked with those of Ruff. He slowly put his rifle aside without being told. "Don't hurt her, mister. She's all I got."

"I'm not going to hurt her." Ruff gave the girl a shove between the shoulderblades, and she tottered forward, glaring back over her shoulder at Ruff.

"Damn this cave rat!" Caleb Waters sputtered, rising from a box of tinned goods. The entire alcove was cluttered with crates and cans, sacks and loose bundles. Ruff seemed not to hear Waters. He looked at the old man.

"Mind telling me what this is about?" Ruff had eased back a little, moving toward the opening which led into the alcove. He could see nothing out there, but the sound of anyone approaching should be audible. His own bootheels had rung clearly, echoing down the long stony corridors.

"Well?" The old man had not answered. He stood, hands hanging, fingertips curled inward, head thrust forward. Whiskers wreathed his narrow face and old, dark eyes sparkled. The girl, her back still to Ruff, looked up into his face.

"I'll tell you, I'll tell you!" the old man said excitedly as if someone had suddenly wound him up. His arms jerked out dramatically as he gestured at Waters and Abigail, who looked cool, sullen, somehow sexy in a long woolen coat, her sleek dark hair knotted back, emphasizing her magnificent facial bones.

"Would you get to it, then?" Ruff asked tolerantly. The old man had said nothing—except that he would say something. "Like where we are, why we are here, who you are, why you have these people prisoner . . . any little thing like that."

"I'll tell you, I'll tell you!" The arm began jerking again. Virginia gripped one of his wrists, and he seemed to calm. He nodded and smiled at the girl. "Everything you want to know. But—you're telling me you're not with them." His head tilted toward Waters and Abigail. "You don't already know?"

"I'm not with them," Ruff assured the man.

"All right then. All right! I'm Caleb Waters," the old man said.

"You're . . ." Ruff shook his head. He looked at the narrow old man, at the young woman who was clutching his arm. "She says she's your daughter and that her name is Haynes."

"Adopted daughter. Adopted—my sister's baby. My sister was taken by the pox, her and her husband both. I took Virginia for my own, but it didn't seem right to change the girl's name, you see." He paused. "But I am Caleb Waters. Bet you, I am."

"Then . . ." Now Ruff couldn't shut him up.

"So I heard this man saying he was Caleb Waters." A gnarled finger jabbed in the direction of the man Ruff knew as Caleb Waters. "Heard it, and I knew he was the one. Then I heard her"—he indicated Abigail, who looked only bored—"and I knew she was with him. Guess they knew I had a daughter and tried to make it look right."

"You were going to—"

Again the old man, now highly agitated, interrupted Ruff. "I bought me a sutler's license, come here to set up shop, I did—look around you, son! Them's my goods. Damned if I was going to let a bunch of savage Sioux chase me away from my investment. I started bringing my goods down into the Honeycomb here while everybody else was packing up to—"

"Wait!" Ruff's expression grew intent. "Honeycomb. This is what you call the cave?"

"Not what I call it—what it's always been called. Honeycomb, on account of the way it's carved out. Limestone it is, and water is what done it. A million years of water. There's ten thousand chambers down here, and no one knows where they all lead, how far it goes. I wouldn't dare go no further than right here, though others have tried—some haven't ever come back. John Zukor was the man who discovered these caves and named 'em. He brought up all sorts of Indian bones and such from deep down. But once he went and didn't return. Folks say the Indian haunts got him—spirits, that is."

Ruff had to hold up a hand. The man's voice rattled on, veering this way and that at the slightest nudge. "Back to the main point," he suggested.

"Sure. It's this—this fellow here knew I was sutler in Grizzly . . . well, that I *would* be if the army ever got to its feet and established that post they've been promising since Crook took command up north . . ."

"Please?"

"He found out. Figured I'd pulled off with my girl. Figured to take my place."

That was concise and illuminating. Also, to judge by the caved-in expression on the other Caleb Waters's face, absolutely true.

Abigail inexplicably burst out into laughter. Virginia spun toward her. "What's so funny, lady? A person like you! You come in and try to steal my pa's chance to make a decent living. What were you going to do if you found out we were alive, that we hadn't run away from

Grizzly, that we still had sutler's rights? Kill us." Virginia went closer, bent slightly forward, "Well—what's so funny?"

"Go away, child," Abigail said with the utmost disdain.

"Waters?" Ruff asked. He was looking at the other man, the one he had known as Caleb Waters. "Whoever you are—true, is it?"

"They said he had disappeared, dammit," was all the fake Waters would say. "Dead and likely the Sioux were using his scalp to decorate their lances. This is the sorriest thing you ever got me into, Abby!"

"Shut up, *Daddy*."

"You," Ruff asked of the real Waters. "What do you plan to do with them now?"

"Damned if I know. All I know is that they're here with twenty men. Who are they? How am I supposed to know who to trust, if anybody? Everyone I knew left Grizzly—smarter than me, I suppose—but I couldn't leave, don't you see? If I pull out the sutlership is open. It's like a gold claim, don't you see?" His eyes, fixed on Ruff, were nearly desperate.

"I do see," Ruff answered.

What Waters said was true, for obvious reasons. The army wanted a sutler, and they would have one. If a man defaulted, then by God the army got another man, and damned soon.

"Question is now," Ruff said slowly, "what the Mac-Adoo gang has to do with this, or with you," he amended, stepping nearer to Waters, the former Waters.

Lanternlight flickered on water-glazed stone behind the man's head. "Oh, God," he moaned. "It was all her. All Abby's doing. She's a vixen, a shrew."

"A rattler?"

"Yes." The fake sutler smiled dimly. "I've known Abby for a good many years. She picked me up in Hibbing when I was down and out. Said she had a scheme going to collect a lucrative sutler's contract—of course, we wouldn't have worked it; we would have sold out for a good profit as soon as possible. We don't even have any

125

goods out there." His eyes lifted toward the surface, toward Grizzly.

What was Thurgood thinking of right now? Ruff wondered. What would all of them think if they knew that there were no blankets, no food stores, no ammunition in those crates Waters had brought?

"She knew MacAdoo?" Ruff asked.

"Yes," the man sighed. "To answer your next questions—yes, she killed Grange. It was, as you guessed, a falling-out among thieves. And yes—she killed Reggie."

Ruff turned his eyes on her, and he could have killed her just then, woman or not. He had run into cool customers before, but this one, she was made of ice. She dared to smile. She rested her fingertips on her breast.

"Why, Abigail, just tell me that?"

"Why, Mr. Justice! Because he found out. Reggie, bizarre creature that he was, was not so very stupid. The night the Sioux hit the camp, Amos MacAdoo had come in to speak to me. Reggie saw us. He heard much."

"And so you bashed his skull in."

"And so . . ." Abigail shrugged, and Ruff stepped toward her. Before he could think about it, weigh it, measure the propriety of it, he had raised his hand and lowered it, slapping her so hard that she was knocked from the packing crate, her cheek stung crimson by the blow, her hair flying. She lay sprawled against the stone floor of the cavern, Ruff Justice standing over her.

"I can't see how that could be necessary," Virginia Haynes said hotly.

"She killed a friend of mine."

"But she's a woman!"

"And she takes every advantage of it. Abigail," Ruff said, "you've made a mistake. Everyone here heard you admit that you killed him. I don't think there's ever been a woman hung in Dakota, but I'm going to try my damnedest to see that you're the first."

"I don't know what right you think you have . . ." Abigail still sat on the floor of the cavern alcove, flushed furiously.

"I may have forgotten to mention that I'm a deputy marshal working out of Bismarck," Ruff answered. He fished in his trouser pocket and showed them all the badge. "Maybe that doesn't give me the right to do much, but I think it gives me the right to take you in. Or," he went on, "if that's impossible, to arrest you in the name of the territorial government and see that you're tried by twelve chosen men."

The color had washed out of Abigail's face. She sat white and angry, her lip curled up at the corner, staring at Justice. Virginia was staring just as hard. She had taken off her hat, and a mass of curly hair spilled down across her shoulders and throat now. Those big blue eyes were impenetrable.

"And what will you do with us?" Caleb Waters finally asked. The lanternlight colored his white whiskers yellow and deepened the hollows of his eyes.

"Do? What should I do? You come on up out of this hole and we'll straighten things out."

"No." Waters's voice was firm.

"No?" Ruff squinted at the old man, trying to make him out. "Why not, Waters?"

"How do we know what's going to happen? How do we know which of those people up there are in his"—a finger poked the air in the direction of the imposter—"employ? Do you know? Tell me, Marshal Tuffin . . ."

Abigail tittered, and Ginny smiled. Ruff sighed.

"Justice," he corrected.

"Mr. Justice," Waters went on, "those could all be this man's hired accomplices."

"Not likely, is it? They'd be cutting the pie too many ways."

"All right. Perhaps there's only one, or two. Enough to sneak up behind you and cut your throat. Then what happens to Virginia and me? No, sir." He wagged his head. "I'm for staying down here, with them under my eyes. You can see we've got supplies enough to last years."

"Fine," Ruff said tautly, "but I'm not spending years

down in this sinkhole. Nor are my prisoners. Nor"—he looked at Ginny—"is this young woman. If her health—"

The distant shot echoed faintly, and Ruff's head turned. He cocked his ear and frowned, listening. Another shot. And another. Then a barrage, a mad, lengthy exchange of shots, all distant, muffled by stone and earth.

"What is it?" Waters demanded. "What's happening up there?" They all looked at the cave ceiling. The shots continued unabated.

"Ta-Shaka's found us," Ruff said grimly.

12

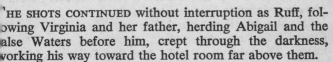

THE SHOTS CONTINUED without interruption as Ruff, following Virginia and her father, herding Abigail and the false Waters before him, crept through the darkness, working his way toward the hotel room far above them.

Ruff heard a whimpering, a broken, nearly sobbing breathing, and he thought at first that it was Abigail. But it proved to be the weaker of the two thieves—the phony Caleb Waters. His nerve was completely gone now.

The cavern itself could do that, Ruff decided. Dark, ominous, it stretched out in all directions like a many-legged, hollow beast. It seemed that they had taken too many turns, come too far, and he yanked back on the old man's shoulder.

"This isn't the way we came."

"No." The hand holding the lantern gestured ahead. "It comes out in the same place. The other way's too steep."

Ruff had no choice but to accept that. Water seeped underfoot, and by the lamplight he could see high vaulted ceilings, mysterious tunnels leading off at unexpected angles, a streak of dead white against the black basaltic ceiling of the cave. He wished he knew more about geology, more about how the earth uptilts and buckles, how water and flowing lava carve out such sepulchers in the earth.

"Hold it!" The old man had stopped, Ginny at his

shoulder, peering anxiously ahead, and Ruff, listening knew they were near to the surface.

They could still hear, indistinctly, the popping of firearms, but there was another, more intimidating noise which caught their attention and held it, lifting pulses.

"What is that?" Abigail asked, looking uncertain for the first time.

It was a roaring, thundering sound like a herd of stampeding buffalo passing overhead. They exchanged glances. No one would hazard a guess.

"Let's have a look," Ruff said. He squeezed past the old man and placed his hand on the hidden panel which led into the hotel room. Lifting his Colt, he slammed his boot against the panel, expecting most anything from a Sioux war lance to a load of buckshot.

It was worse than either. The panel flew open and the flames leaped out toward Ruff. Smoke billowed into the cavern. The heat was intense, and Ruff fell back, his arm across his face.

Abigail, revealing emotion and plenty of it now, screamed, "Trapped! Trapped down here! God!"

"Shut up," Ginny said. Then reasonably: "There's nothing hysterics can do to help us out of this."

The flames still stretched out hungry red fingers toward them, and the smoke clouded the stony corridor. They backed away from the panel, watching as timber caved into the tunnel. For one brief moment before the flaming curtain was drawn across his vision, Ruff had been able to see a starlit sky—the roof of the hotel was completely gone. Likely all of Grizzly would be burned to the ground by morning.

"Get back," he told them all. "We'll have to stay down until it burns itself out and then go up another way."

"Another way?" the old man chuckled. "Mister, if there's another way, I know nothing about it."

Abigail wailed again. Ruff glanced at her, amazed at this crack in her composure. She stood there beautiful, stunned, smudged, and he had to remind himself what a cold-blooded she-wolf she was.

"Well, what's the problem?" the fake Waters asked. "All we have to do is wait for the fire to burn itself out, for the Indians to leave." He waved an arm. "We've got plenty of food, plenty of—"

Before he could finish his sentence, there was a thunderous exposion. Ruff was hurled back against the wall of the tunnel, sprawling against Ginny. Flame shot into the cave and then was snuffed out as a thousand tons of stone collapsed.

The roof of the cavern caved in, showering them with stone and dust. The lantern went out and the rumblings shook the earth. Ruff was on his back, Ginny on top of him. They peered with anxious eyes into the darkness, but there was nothing they could see. The darkness was vast and complete.

"Pa!" Ginny pushed herself away from Justice and clawed her way toward the enormous, unseen pile of rubble. "Pa!" Her voice was frantic and shrill.

"Find him?" Ruff asked. There was no answer. "Abigail?" Again no answer. "Waters?"

"My God, they're all dead, all dead!" Ginny screamed. Ruff got to his knees. Stone dust sifted down over him. Creeping forward, he touched Ginny's hand. She was digging frantically at the pile of stone.

"Settle down," Ruff told her. "We don't know that anyone's dead. Let's see if we can't find that lantern first."

"My Pa's under there, dying!"

"You're not going to have much luck in the dark!" Ruff said more harshly than he intended. He began feeling around, searching for the lantern, but he couldn't find it. "Is there another one back in your cubbyhole?"

"Yes, but I can't leave—"

"Do you know the way? In the dark?"

"Yes, but—"

"Dammit, get going then. I'll start clearing away some of the rocks." There was complete silence. "Ginny? Are you there?"

"Yes." The voice came out of the darkness. "I'm going."

He listened to her departing footsteps and then turned to work on the pile of rocks. He proceeded cautiously—not being able to see anything at all, he was wary of pulling a key rock free, of being crushed by a second cave-in.

Overhead the gunshots continued sporadically. They were extremely faint now. Ruff was perspiring freely. Dust clung to his body and clotted his nostrils. He touched the hand without seeing it.

Still warm, but lifeless, limp. He touched the wrist with his fingertips and felt no pulse. Shifting a few rocks, he touched the coat sleeve. Homespun broadcloth. Ginny's father. He swallowed a curse and continued to work.

Aware of a dim glow behind him, Ruff looked across his shoulder, watching as Ginny approached. Her face turned to a mask of sudden horror, her eyes wide, mouth open. She managed to gurgle something, and Ruff, looking up, saw the roof of the cavern start to collapse once again.

This time it was as if the entire town of Grizzly were falling. The earth shook beneath their feet. Ruff bolted, grabbing Ginny's arm, as the trembling became a roar and a thousand tons of fresh material sagged down to cover the exit to the tunnel.

She trembled, started forward, trying to fight free of Ruff's arms, and then gave it up.

"Now I'll never know," she said, looking dismally at the pile of rock.

"He might have gotten through to the other side," Ruff said, trying to comfort her. "It was dark. I couldn't see what happened."

"You're kind, aren't you?" she said with surprise.

"What do you mean?"

"I know he's under there, Mister Justice. I saw him go down under the rock. I just meant . . . I wanted to know he wasn't alive, still suffering, hoping . . ."

"You don't have to worry about that," Ruff told her. Those huge blue eyes looked up at him, and she gripped his arm tightly.

"It's all right," she said at the look of concern on

Ruff's face. "It's just that I wanted to know. I'm the kind of woman who needs to be told the truth. I can handle it."

"Sure."

Then she collapsed against him, her face buried against his chest, her body shaking convulsively. She pulled away abruptly, keeping her eyes turned from him, ashamed of her emotional display.

"The shots—they've stopped," Ginny said, looking up at the dark ceiling of the cave.

"That or we just can't hear them anymore," Ruff responded. "There's a lot of rock between the street and us."

"Can we . . . dig our way through?"

He shook his head. "Not in a year."

"Then what are we going to do?" she asked, not whiningly, but simply to discover what there was to be done. Ruff found himself liking this tough little woman. She had lost her parents, lost her adopted father. Now, trapped in this stony pit, she wasn't about to cry or raise a scene.

"There has to be another way out."

"Pa never found one. Neither did I. Of course, he wouldn't let me go too far into the Honeycomb. It's endless, you know—or nearly so. A person could get trapped, lost, and . . ."

That was exactly their position now. They had food and light and could survive for a while. But survive to what end? No help would ever arrive—no one knew they were down there. Ruff wasn't cut out to be a mole.

"We're going to have to try it, Ginny. Try to find a way. To sit here is to die."

"I know it." She looked away from the light down the endless labyrinthine corridors. She nodded her head decisively and said, "We'll have to see what supplies we can use."

She led off toward the alcove where Caleb Waters had stored his supplies, where he had come to be safe from Indian attack. Neither of them talked about the task

133

ahead of them. A dangerous, probably foolish task, one which offered no promise of a successful completion.

There was only the cave, the long dark, winding tunnels leading down into the heart of the earth. If there was a way out no one had ever found it. What would it do to a man, Ruff wondered, to slowly lose his way, to feel hope slipping away, to spend day after day searching endless corridors for a way out which did not exist?

"Here we are." Ginny placed the lantern on a crate and stood back. She hunched her shoulders helplessly. The light played on her long, wavy hair, streaking it with golden highlights.

"Blankets," Ruff told her. "Two each. One can be used to carry supplies in."

Ginny nodded her head, shaking off the lethargy. She opened a packing crate and pulled out four blankets. Ruff spread one out on the floor to roll his supplies in, and she did the same.

Keep her busy, he told himself. Keep her mind off it. How long could he hope to do that? Nevertheless, he tried.

"What sorts of tinned food do you have?"

"There's corned beef. Peaches?" She read the labels. Ruff nodded, and she tossed the cans to him.

"Is there any rope, Ginny?"

"Plenty of it."

It would be heavy, but he wanted as much as he could tote. In the end he took fifty feet of new hemp, coiled to be carried over his shoulder.

"And matches. Fill up all the lanterns we have with coal oil." The darkness was one thing Ruff didn't want to risk. "A bar of soap, too."

"Plan on taking a bath?"

"I was figuring on marking the walls of the cave as we went."

"How about this?" She produced chalk from inside one of the boxes. "Pa uses it . . . to tally on a blackboard."

"Fine." Ruff stood, feeling a little light-headed. There was dust still sifting through the air, and he wondered with abrupt concern if there wasn't less oxygen in the cavern now.

Rolling up his blanket, Ruff tied the ends together; slinging it over his shoulder like a horseshoe, he tied it again, placing the bulky rope on top of it.

"Ready?" he asked.

"Not much," Ginny answered, and surprisingly she managed to laugh. Ruff smiled in return.

"Have you any ideas?"

"Well, only that we don't go right. That passage is a dead end about fifty feet on."

Then it was to the left. Stepping out of the alcove, Ruff held his lantern high and looked that way. The way down was only a path winding along the wall of the cave. Below, somewhere, water ran—it was far below. Ruff kicked a stone over and counted five before it hit.

"Here we go. Take it easy, Ginny."

She nodded, parted her lips to say something, and found her mouth too dry to speak. Ruff led off along the face of the dark cavern wall.

The trail was three feet wide, narrowing as it made a tight downward bend, then widening some again as it burrowed into the heart of the earth.

Ruff's attention was totally on the trail ahead of him. He saw it only in five-foot sections as the flickering lantern illuminated the narrow shelf.

Water seeped out of the walls and ran across the ledge, making it treacherous, and twice Ruff almost went over. It was cold inside the Honeycomb, and it grew colder as they crept forward.

"Look there," Ginny said, her voice echoing. Ruff saw what she meant—a branch tunnel led off the cliff face. Holding the lantern aloft, Ruff examined it. "Well?" the girl asked, clinging to his arm.

"I don't know. It leads up, anyway. If we hope to get out of here, I've an idea we'd better not go down any farther than necessary."

"You're right. Water carved this, didn't it? Part of it, anyway. There must be a way for water to get down."

135

"Sure," Ruff agreed, hardly convinced. The air was musty at this depth, and there was a stench rising up from the depths, like rotting vegetable matter. It seemed to come from the green-gray lichen which clung to the surface of the stone cavern. "Up it is, then," he said, shifting the coil of rope on his shoulder.

This way was a narrow tunnel, nearly oval-shaped, the ceiling at about eight feet. There was much loose stone underfoot, which lifted Ginny's spirits—she claimed that water must have washed it down from above. Ruff encouraged her optimism.

As they made their way up the gradually inclining tunnel, Ruff marked the walls of the cave with large X's. If they reached a dead end, he wanted at least to be able to get back to the alcove where there were more supplies to be had.

The tunnel took a sudden upward turn, and Ginny paused, waiting for him. She stood panting, looking up the dark, narrowing passage.

"We'll have to try it," Ruff said. "Want me to go first?"

"No. I can do it." She wiped her hair back, smiled, and started up. The tunnel narrowed still more as they rounded the first bend on hands and knees. How deep were they? Was the girl right in supposing there would be an entrance hole?

Ruff's fingers clawed at the rock now. He had to wedge himself in to keep from sliding back. There was no purchase at all. Ginny was game, but she was tiring badly. He saw the determination on her smudged face, and he hoped he wouldn't have to see it turn to eventual despair.

"I think . . ." she puffed. "Yes, there's some sort of ledge up here. If you could boost me."

Ruff hung his lantern on his belt, braced himself, and put a hand on Ginny's boot. Straining, he lifted as high as he could. He felt her struggling to draw herself up onto the ledge. Rocks bounded down through the bleak tunnel, ringing off the walls. "I'm up," she said triumphantly, rolling out of sight.

He saw her face peering downward from out of a hidden alcove, saw her gesturing hand, and he began climbing again, inching his way up, bracing his feet against one side of the chute, his shoulders against the other.

Finally, groping overhead, Ruff was able to touch Ginny's hand and then to find the lip of the ledge. He pulled himself up and over, finding himself beside the girl in an alcove which was six feet wide but no more than four high.

By the lanternlight Ruff could see that the shaft continued upward at a more gradual angle. Black basaltic rock, gleaming coldly in the light, encircled them.

Ginny shivered. "Brr."

"Cold?"

"It's not that—I don't like close places much."

"No." Especially not a hundred feet underground. "Think this is the way?" he asked.

"Well—we're here. We're still going up, aren't we? Let's have a look."

"Lead on."

She did, crawling forward, rounding a curved bend in the trail, creeping upward. "It branches," Ginny called over her shoulder. Ruff wiped the perspiration from his eyes and moved up to look past her at the Y in the tunnel.

"Which one?"

"This one." She nodded at the left-hand trail. "It continues upward and it's a little wider."

"Go ahead," Ruff answered. He placed a big X on the wall at the juncture and followed the girl. Despite himself, he caught his eyes fixing on the round strength of her haunches as she crawled ahead of him. She was quite a girl, this one. Unafraid—or no more afraid than anyone would be. Determined, proud.

She was also, at certain angles, amazingly stirring.

"Branches again," Ginny puffed. The air was very stale in the shaft now as the sides of the tunnel crept in to close around them. Craning his neck, Ruff could see a three-way split of the corridor. He breathed a curse—the

137

ceiling was growing lower. Whichever way they went, it appeared they would have to crawl.

"Choose one," he said. Ginny hesitated a moment before starting off, going nearly flat, pushing the lantern ahead of her, scraping knees and elbows, squeezing upward, upward, where somewhere there had to be fresh air, sunlight, grass and trees . . .

"Branch," she said, and her voice was close to desperation. "Ruff, I think the one to the right widens out a little."

"All right." That didn't make it the right way—if there was a right way; Ruff didn't wish to dwell on that—but it made it possible to proceed. The way they were going now they would soon run out of room to do anything but wriggle their toes.

Ruff's body ached. His legs were cramped, his arms knotted with the effort. He could only imagine how the girl felt. But she didn't complain.

She moved ahead more quickly now, with an energy which suggested desperation. Once when she turned her head the right way Ruff could see her face, see the tautness in it, the set of her mouth, the wide eyes. No, she didn't like close places, and she was liking it less every moment.

They crawled fifty feet down a funnel-shaped tunnel which opened slightly and then turned up to end in a kind of shelf of limestone where trickling, mineral-laden water had formed weird stalactites and stalagmites like a bed of nails. The lanternlight danced across these forms, causing them to waver and bend, to jump into sharp, angry relief. It was enough to jolt the imagination.

"I . . ." Ginny was panting roughly.

"Take it easy. Sit and rest," he told her. "We've earned it."

She nodded. Ruff unshouldered his blanket and rope. Rubbing the raw muscle of neck and shoulder, he sat on the cold, bizarre ledge beside the girl, glancing around him at the stalactites which seemed like the teeth in the jaws of a monster fish ready to snap shut on them.

"It's cold," Ginny said, and Ruff put his arm around her, drawing her to him. "I can't see a way," she said, looking around the cavern, which was thirty feet wide by twenty high. A stack of rocks lay against the cold whitish floor.

"We'll find one."

"I brought us all this way for nothing. It was the wrong way."

"Yes." He squeezed her shoulder. "But we'll find the right way. We'll work our way back down after we've gotten our breath."

"And try another tunnel." She rubbed her face with a small hand. "And then another, and another!"

She buried her face in the hollow of his shoulder, and he held her tightly for a moment, murmuring small reassurances. She was starting to come apart. Well, let her get it over with now.

"Let's get some sleep," he suggested.

"Here?" she nearly shrieked.

"Do you prefer another cave?" he asked lightly. "Ginny, we won't get far if we're exhausted. We've got blankets and food. We'll get out. But there's no point in wearing ourselves out."

She was nodding her head, but she seemed not to hear him. "I don't want to eat," she answered finally. "But I think I can sleep." She smiled weakly.

The floor of the cavern was broken and cold. Stony teeth projected upward. Ruff found a place to make their beds, however. Ginny seemed unwilling to lie down and sleep—Ruff didn't really blame her. The place, the situation, if dwelled upon was enough to shake anyone.

Still, she was fairly composed until he gave her the word: "We'll have to have the lanterns out."

"In here!" Her face was contorted by fear. She waved an arm toward the toothy stones overhead, the damp, creeping stillness of the cavern.

"There's not much choice. We haven't got coal oil to spare. We don't need the light while we're sleeping."

"But it's like sleeping . . . in Hades."

Not much different, Ruff reflected. Nevertheless, that was the way it was going to have to be. He couldn't waste the lantern fuel. To have any hope of surviving, they needed those lanterns. He couldn't give in, much as the terror in the girl's eyes tempted him to.

"All right." She turned in a helpless circle. "It's dark with your eyes closed anyway." Ruff offered a meager smile which she couldn't answer. Ginny lay down finally, curling up in her blanket, which did little to keep out the seeping chill of this place.

When she was settled, eyes closed tightly, Ruff stepped to his own blankets and turned the lantern out. The blackness was sudden and complete, unlike any which exists on the surface. There there was always feeble starlight, glimmerings of gray light, even on the darkest nights. Nothing like this. Nothing. The darkness seemed to have weight, to lie on a man and crush him. Hades was no whimsical description.

He could hear Ginny breathing beside him, and it was much too rapid. He almost relented and lit the lantern, but he could not. Survival depended on it. Maybe, he thought grimly, a man could get used to this.

He closed his eyes and tried to sleep. Tiny pinpricks of light seemed to dance brightly in his skull—red, yellow, white. He opened his eyes only to find the darkness greater, and then, with a sigh, he rolled to his side, curled up, and tried to force sleep to come.

It was half an hour later when he heard the soft sobbing and then the touch of a hand against his chest. Ruff lifted the corner of his blanket and she came in beside him, clinging to him like a panicked child.

He stroked her soft hair and hugged her tightly. Her voice was blurred, fragmented.

"I hope you don't think . . . I don't. I wouldn't want you to think . . ."

"I don't think anything," Ruff replied.

He felt her shift. Although his eyes were open, he saw nothing. No shadow, nothing. He felt warm, moist lips

140

against his, felt warm liquid run across his cheek, tasted the salt of her tear.

He held her, and she lay still for a time, still shuddering. It was cold and empty—it was like being alone in the world. The fingers which stretched out, the hands which ran across his chest and unbuttoned his shirt, seemed to be disembodied. The mouth tight against his, the weight and warmth of flesh belonged to no one.

His shirt was off and then his trousers as deft fingers moved across him. There was no spoken word, only soft intent caresses searching him, finding him.

When he rolled to her she was naked, all invisible warmth and lustiness. Her breasts were gifts of the darkness, her thigh brushing against his seemed dreamlike. But there was substance to her. Her breath was next to his ear. Her hands guiding him between her thighs were eager and certain.

She lay back with a sigh and Ruff was pressed against her, feeling the slight tremors in her thighs, her belly become thrusting, deliberate motion as her hips lifted and swayed, pitched and rolled against him, swallowing him, devouring him as the darkness became a magnificent thing—deep black velvet plush and rich, ripe with gentle murmurings and probing fingers, with a sudden bursting warmth.

It flared up with brilliant lights, surrounded Ruff with warm contentment, reached an explosive heat which crackled like a hearth fire and drove away demons.

And then it stilled, becoming slow gentle breathing, close contentment, quiet and deeply complete. They slept.

13

·····➤◆►····

RUFF AWOKE SLOWLY, feeling drugged with the night of love, the exertions of the previous day, the lack of clean air.

It was a long time after he had opened his eyes to the utter blackness of the cavern before he could recall where he was. For a time, in half-sleeping imagination, he had decided that he had been buried, that this was what it was like in the grave. Someone had caught up with him—a bullet in the skull while he slept, perhaps. His last risk had been played, and he had lost.

Then he was aware of the weight of a body against his and he knew he was not dead. Not unless the bosses of the underworld provided the dead with warm young women with sleep-tangled limbs. That seemed unlikely, and gradually the fog cleared away.

He was awake now, but it was a dawn such as he had never known. Black dawn, black world, empty thing. He didn't want to rise, to turn on the lantern. He wanted to roll to the woman, to tumble with her again and again, to waste the day away in lovemaking.

That would do nothing to save their lives.

"Ginny?" He shook her bare shoulder, pausing to give it a small kiss.

"Yes," she answered through a yawn.

"Morning." Or evening, or midnight . . . anyway, it

142

was time to rise. She didn't respond to his announcement. Her breathing seemed to halt, in fact, and he knew she was lying coldly awake now, staring out at the empty, total blackness. Maybe he should have lighted the lantern first.

"All right," she said eventually. "Can't we please have some light?"

"I wasn't sure you'd want me to see you until you'd dressed," he answered.

That brought a laugh from Ginny's lips. A wholehearted, genuinely cheerful laugh. "If I can have light, Ruff Justice, I don't care if the whole world is watching."

It wasn't the whole world, but there was one man who watched as the lantern under the influence of a red-glowing match flared to life. And he watched with deep appreciation.

A small woman was Ginny, but perfectly proportioned. Her legs were slender, the muscle tone excellent beneath flawless skin. Her hips flared out in a promise of genial competence. Her breasts rode high and full.

She caught his eyes on her, and her eyes flashed with an expression Ruff couldn't measure—anger, pride, excitement, embarrassment. All or none of these. She coolly dressed, and Ruff, sighing, pulled on his buckskins, stamping into his boots.

"Breakfast?" he asked.

"What have we got?"

"Most anything you like. If you like salt biscuits, corned beef, and tinned peaches."

"Anything sounds good this morning. I'm so hungry . . ." Her voice fell away, and this time it was definitely embarrassment. Ruff grinned.

The lanternlight played on her hair, on her breasts, casting weaving, indistinct shadows around the cavern walls. The yawning jaws of the toothy cave flickered in the light. Ruff, using his Bowie, opened the tins of food.

When Ginny was dressed she crouched down beside Ruff, eating the salty tinned meat, the salt biscuits silently.

She had begun thinking about it again, and it was no good to do that.

Most of the morning would have to be spent returning to where they had been yesterday—if this was morning and that was yesterday—to choose another tunnel, to try again to fight their way out of this gloomy, suffocating pit.

When Ginny had finished her meal she tossed the cans aside, picked up her pack, and said, "No sense feeling sorry for myself—let's have at it, Mr. Justice."

"That's better," he said, placing his hands on her shoulders, kissing the tip of her small nose.

"What?"

"You at least know my name now."

"I know a lot more about you after last night," she said, kissing him in return. "I don't think we've got the time for that right now, do we?"

"I don't think so."

They made their way back through the narrow tunnel on hands and knees. The shaft downward was a problem, and once Ruff skidded blindly through the darkness, tearing hands and knees as he tried to apply the brakes.

Finally, pausing for breath in the dust-choked darkness, he sat down and waited for Ginny. Glancing up, he saw it . . . or didn't see it. He stood, eyes fixed on the wall of the cavern. He placed his hand against the stone, not turning his head as Ginny slid down in a shower of stone and dust.

"What . . . what is it, Ruff?" she inquired, leaning her head around to smile hesitantly up at him. The smoky shadows cast by the lantern flickered across Ruff's face. It was hard-set, wooden.

"Nothing. Only—I could swear this was where I put my mark."

"The X?"

"That's right. So we wouldn't take the wrong turn."

"Well, you must be mistaken." Her forehead furrowed in an expression of worry. "Could there be water seeping through? That would wash it away, wouldn't it?"

"Dry as a bone," Ruff said, running his hand down the stone.

"Well, then it has to be the wrong place."

"Yes," Ruff told her. All the same, he was uneasy, and he shifted his rope and blanket roll so that he had easier access to his gun.

They returned down the dark passage which led to the hairline trail above the sinkhole. Or Ruff thought that was the way they were taking. Fifty feet on, he turned and said, "This can't be the way. None of my marks anywhere."

"I'm sure it is the way," Ginny answered in a tone which indicated she was anything but sure. They went on. They passed a branch tunnel, low, gaping, and another high and narrow. Ruff looked everywhere for his chalkmarks, finding none.

"It's got to be this way," Ginny said.

"I think we should go back."

"Back! Back where?" she said in utter frustration. She sniffed and recovered herself. "I'm sure this is the way."

Ruff wasn't, but he followed her ahead, down the winding smooth-walled tunnel which now widened somewhat. Ginny stopped abruptly.

"What's the matter?"

"Did you hear that?" She gripped his sleeve. "A voice. I'm sure of it."

"A voice?" Ruff's eyes narrowed. He wiped the sweat from his forehead—the temperature was over a hundred. "Are you sure?"

Ginny parted her lips, began to speak, and then seemed to collapse inwardly. "No—I'm not sure! This tomb is driving me insane. I hear voices murmuring everywhere, I..."

"Ginny." Ruff took her by the shoulders, forced her to look up into his eyes. "This won't help."

"No," she said, managing a smile. She wiped her long hair from her face. "This won't help."

The dead man was around the next bend.

Long dead, although he had been preserved by the

dryness of the Honeycomb. He sat grinning up at them from a yellowed, leathery skull. Ginny screamed, and Ruff winced. He went forward and poked at the mummy with his boot toe. The head rolled off the shoulders, and Ginny screamed again, her voice broken, tragic.

"Who . . . ?" she asked.

"John Zukor, I would think," Ruff said. Beside the man was an ancient pistol, an empty rucksack. The discoverer of the Honeycomb, the man who had never returned from its vaults, lay before them, and the warning wasn't lost on Ruff and Ginny. This was the man who had known this cavern better than anyone. He hadn't made it back.

"Forget it; let's keep moving," Ruff said sharply. Ginny nodded like a zombie.

"But he, but he . . ."

"He ran out of food, that's all," Ruff growled. "We won't. Get moving!" He actually shoved her until she went ahead. There were five different shafts leading out of this chamber, and there was no way of choosing between them.

The lanternlight bled across the walls, now white limestone again, smooth as glass, water-polished. Something scuttled away underfoot, and Ruff watched it. Pure-white, blind, a translucent gecko, a lizard whose ancestors had come into the cave and over the eons had become sightless, needing no eyes. Ruff wondered vaguely what would happen to a race of men trapped underground in this blackness for eternity.

Ginny screamed, and he saw her go down. It was as if the ground had swallowed her up. A thunder of pint-sized bats swept past Ruff, and he covered his face, fighting to where Ginny had gone over.

He nearly stepped into the vertical shaft before he saw it. Panicked by the swarming bats, she had looked up instead of down. It was dark in the hole. Ruff cursed, knowing they had lost a lantern.

"All right?"

It was too long before she answered. "Yes, I think so. Just an ankle." *Just an ankle.* Ruff cursed inwardly.

"All right. I'm going to drop the rope. Gather up what supplies you can find without moving from where you are. Don't move, got it?" For all they knew there was another drop-off down there.

The rope vanished into the maw of the pit, and he waited. "Can you feel the rope?"

"I can't. Wait a minute. All right."

It was another minute while she tied it on according to Ruff's instructions and he brought her up, hand over hand, his shoulders aching.

Finally, panting and dirty, she emerged from the pit and sagged to the stone floor, holding her ankle. "Broken?" Ruff asked.

"I don't think so." But she could not support her weight, and Ruff, not for the first time, breathed a slow curse. "I . . . I'm sorry," she said.

"Nothin' to worry about. I'll tote you."

"But you can't!"

"Sure I can—don't get silly about it. I'll give you a minute's rest. Meantime . . ." He unshouldered his pack.

"What are you going to do?" she asked almost in panic.

"Go down and have a look. Most of our supplies are down there."

He tied onto a rocky outcropping, checking his knot twice, testing his weight as Ginny watched him with those wide blue eyes. Then, grinning, he tied the lantern to his belt, dropped over the edge of the pit, and was gone.

Bracing his boots against the side of the shaft, Ruff eased down, the swaying lantern casting wavering shadows. Below he caught the glint of metal, formless and dim. He could not see the bottom of the shaft, however. Ginny had taken quite a tumble, but had she missed the narrow tongue of stone where she had landed, it would have been a tumble into eternity.

"If you can . . ." Ruff called up. That was all he said.

The rope came slack in his hands and he was falling, falling through what seemed limitless space.

Suddenly it was not limitless. Stone slammed into Ruff's body, driving the wind from his lungs, the consciousness from his skull, and he continued to fall, down a spinning velvety tunnel which led into the bowels of the earth, beyond, into Hades, while mocking faces, all white and sightless, laughed.

Awakening was unreality. The world was dark and cold. Where was he? In a place where pain dominated; pain and infinite blackness.

Ruff shook his head, started to rise, and fell on his face with a jolt as his hand found no place to rest. Feeling carefully with stiff fingers, he discovered why. He was lying on the very edge of the stony ledge where Ginny had been earlier. But how?

The rope had broken.

That rope? Brand-new three-quarter-inch hemp? Not likely. All right then—she cut it.

Ginny? Ruff shook his head. Not Ginny. What reason could she possibly have? *But there was no one else in the cave!*

There was, of course. Ruff knew it now as he had suspected it all along. Reggie had tried to tell him that there was a perfect hiding place near Grizzly: in the Honeycomb. And they were in here somewhere. Amos MacAdoo and Tug Slaussen.

Now they had Ginny, and that was enough to start the blood pounding in Ruff's aching head. They had Ginny and he was trapped in this pit in utter darkness. One thought buoyed his spirits somewhat—there was a very good chance that there was another way out of this stony labyrinth. MacAdoo and Slaussen hadn't snuck past Caleb Waters and Ginny, or at least that seemed unlikely. There was a way!

A lot of good it was going to do Justice. Bracing himself, he rose clumsily. He could feel the side of the shaft and he knew where the ledge ended. That was all he

148

knew, and it seemed that standing up was all he was going to accomplish.

Shaking away the negative thoughts, Ruff tried to think. It hurt his head. He could feel a lump the size of a walnut on his skull, feel the trickle of blood. His shoulder ached horribly, and one knee was torn up pretty bad.

He ran his fingers over the face of the cliff, discovering immediately that he wasn't going to climb it. It was as smooth as a mirror. His foot found the snarled coil of rope, and he picked it up; searching fingers confirmed that the end had been cut.

The darkness was enough to drive him batty, and he decided to light a precious match, although he wasn't so damned sure they weren't still up there, waiting. Illuminated by a match glow he would make a dandy target—fish in a rain barrel.

The matchhead scraped with Ruff's thumbnail flared to life, and he flinched. The light was glaring. It was incredible that the tiny flame could blind a man, but everything below ground was incredible. By the light he saw his lantern and Ginny's—both smashed and useless.

Well . . . maybe. Ruff crouched down, burning his fingers on the match. Lighting another, he shook the lanterns. Both had a fair amount of coal oil left. Finding Ginny's blanket roll, he used his knife to cut the blanket to strips. Laying the strips out, he soaked them in coal oil. His Spencer, lying at his feet, completed the makeshift invention.

Winding the soaked blanket strips around the muzzle of the rifle, he knotted them firmly. It would do for a torch—it would have to.

Knowing he couldn't go up, Ruff considered going downward. Down to what he didn't know. He only knew things couldn't get any worse somewhere other than where he was. He had some food, some light, and an excellent chance of dying on that ledge, mummifying like John Zukor, spending the rest of eternity propped up grinning into darkness.

He could tie on to an outcropping above the ledge, he

discovered by matchlight—six matches left in the tin box—but how far he would have to go he couldn't even guess. He had thirty feet of rope left, and he couldn't see the bottom of the shaft, which fell away vertically at his feet.

Climbing down with his torch was going to be a problem—Ruff decided he couldn't do it. He would have to leave the ledge in darkness and try to find a way out with the unlighted torch slung across his back, ready for use when—if—he found a way out.

He made his preparations. A few cans of tinned food jammed inside his shirt, rifle on a blanket sling in position, rope tied onto the outcropping. Then, peering once more into the pit, he shook his head and had at it.

He locked his boots together around the rope and hand-over-handed it down, groping against the darkness. Nothing. The world was empty and dark and angry. His probing boot toes found nothing on which to brace himself even for a moment. His shoulders ached; he spun slowly through the darkness.

Sweat poured from his face and chest. His hands were raw. Nothing.

He had dropped straight downward, and now with anxiety he realized that the face of the cliff was falling away from him. He could no longer touch stone.

His boots ran out of rope; he was at the limit and had discovered nothing. There was no place to stop, to rest. No way out.

Ruff hung his head; perspiration dripped into his eyes. He chanced groping for a match, one-handing the box open, lighting it with his thumbnail.

It flared up red and yellow, hot and angry, and by the glare Ruff saw one thin hope. By the light it seemed he saw a cave opening up in the side of the sheer face.

The only trouble was it was ten feet lower than Ruff was just now. It would mean lowering himself to the very end of the rope, somehow getting himself into motion, and swinging toward it—for the cliff face was now twenty feet away. Then, assuming he didn't lose his grip and plummet to the bottom of the shaft, smashing himself on the stone floor, he would be stuck. Stuck irremediably on that ledge with no way up or down, since he would have to let go of the rope as it swung through its pendulum motion and hurl himself through the darkness hoping to land on the ledge of this cavern mouth.

If he missed, as seemed likely, he was dead. If he made it, he had no hope at all of ever getting out of the Honeycomb if that yawning shaft dead-ended.

The cramping of his hands, the burning sensation as the rope inched through his grip, decided him. He doubted he could make the climb back up to the first ledge, and assuming he could, there was no hope to be found there. It had to be here, and soon.

Ruff started himself into motion. The sensation of arcing back and forth through the blackness was dizzying and supernatural.

Slowly the pendulous motion increased, and Ruff knew he was getting closer to the edge of the wall. He didn't know how close. He had to strike a match and knew it, yet his grip was loosening constantly. To let go with one hand might be to trigger a rapid, fatal descent. To jump blind was to die.

He pawed a match from his pocket and lit it. The cave mouth was so near that it astonished him. Black, yawning, it threatened to swallow him up.

Without thinking about it he let go of the rope. The match was snuffed out in darkness. Ruff was sailing through blind space. Then he slammed against stone, rolled over, felt his legs going into emptiness, and with desperate effort pulled himself away from the edge of the cavern mouth.

He lay there gasping for breath; his shoulders ached, his hands burned. The world had gone to night again, but his heart raced with excitement. He was on solid earth. Rolling to his knees, Ruff unslung his rifle, struck a match, and touched the oil-soaked rags, which flared to life, illuminating the convoluted cavern where he had landed.

It was wide, gaping, deep—deep enough? No telling. Walking forward, needing to know, almost afraid to know, he moved into the heart of the cavern. His boot-steps echoed back to him; the torch flared hotly: red, bending flames and black billowing smoke.

He crept forward, his feet slowing of their own volition, reluctant to find that the stone wall ahead of him was without break, that he was doomed to spend the rest of his life on that cold ledge.

Holding the torch aloft, he suddenly saw it, and his heart skipped. An opening in the gray stone, a passage, leading . . . ? It didn't have to lead anywhere, of course, but that could be worried about later.

Ruff went nearer and held the torch still higher, examining the opening, which was six feet up, perhaps twelve feet in diameter. He had only to toss his torch up, chin himself, and roll over. He tossed the flaming torch ahead and started to climb. His body froze into motionlessness. The torch still burned brightly. And somewhere ahead—somewhere—he could hear quite distinctly the sound of men's voices.

14

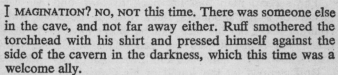

I MAGINATION? NO, NOT this time. There was someone else in the cave, and not far away either. Ruff smothered the torchhead with his shirt and pressed himself against the side of the cavern in the darkness, which this time was a welcome ally.

He thought for a moment that his eyes were betraying him. He saw light, light not of his own making, or the reflection of it. He crept that way, the comforting weight of his Colt in his hand. He knew who it was, who it had to be, and his muscles knotted with eagerness. His hand gripped the handle of the Colt as if to crush it.

He was a cat, feeling his way down the corridor of stone, eyes searching, ears attuned to each small sound. The voices, low, muttering, continued, and now Ruff was near enough that he could make out an occasional word.

"Another week . . . girl'll help." Laughter.

Ruff softly slipped toward the voice. A pebble rolled under his boot, and he froze.

"What was that?"

"Damn bats again, likely."

"It didn't sound like a bat."

"Settle down, Crowder. You've been up that tunnel. You know there's no way anyone could get in."

Crowder grunted, muttered something about the damned Sioux, and then fell silent.

Ruff gave them a good long time to forget about the noise. Standing there, he wondered where Ginny could be. With disgust he realized that one of them could have her off somewhere killing time.

He eased forward again, his head peering around the corner of a firelit tunnel. Two men sat together playing cards on a crate. Two torches burned in wall holders. Beyond the two were more crates, roughly made-up beds, and three saddles. Where were the horses? Which way was out, anyway?

Ruff could see one man's face. Crowder. The description Reggie had given him fit nicely. Crooked, nearly S-shaped nose, his head as bald as an egg.

The second man had his back to him, and he was broad across the shoulders, thick through the chest. Ruff couldn't make out his face, but he didn't have to. A luxuriant red beard flowed out across his shoulders, like flames flowing from his face and throat. Amos MacAdoo.

Ruff stepped in, the sound of his Colt clicking as the hammer was drawn back loud and menacing in the cavern. MacAdoo's hand, reaching for his cards, froze. Crowder jumped.

"Slaussen?" MacAdoo asked without turning his head. Crowder's wide eyes must have already told the big man that it wasn't Tug Slaussen who stood behind him, Colt in hand.

"Afraid not, MacAdoo."

"Justice?"

"That's right." MacAdoo hadn't moved yet. Ruff's eyes were riveted to the big man's hands, to the rifle which rested across the crate between the two men.

"Heard of you," MacAdoo acknowledged, grudgingly it seemed. "Told Slaussen he ought to clamber down and put a bullet in you."

"Where's the girl?" Ruff asked, inching forward, his eyes flickering to the corners of the smoky cavern.

"I don't know," MacAdoo began. Ruff moved directly behind the big man and jammed the muzzle of his Colt under his ear.

"I won't ask again," Ruff hissed.

"Down that tunnel ahead there's a little cave where the river comes through. Slaussen took her up there to give her a bath."

Ruff shoved MacAdoo away from him and, stretching around carefully, reached for the rifle on the table.

MacAdoo was motionless, his hands gripping his thighs. Crowder, panicking, was not so smart. He lunged forward, clawing at Ruff's gunhand. The Colt boomed in the close confines of the cavern and Crowder's chest exploded, spraying them with blood. Still he clung to Ruff's arm with desperate, dying strength.

MacAdoo, picking up the rifle by the barrel, swung it viciously at Ruff's head. The stock glanced off his skull as Ruff managed to duck just in time to keep his head from being crushed. Still it was enough to drop him to his knees, and he got tangled with Crowder's body.

Ruff fired from the floor and MacAdoo spun around, dropping the rifle. Before Ruff could claw his way free of the dead weight of the other outlaw's body, MacAdoo, limping heavily, had torn one torch from the wall and flung it at Ruff's face. Ruff fired again, missing. The ricochets sang a deadly chorus around the stone-walled cavern.

The torch glancing off a hastily upraised forearm had caused his aim to be thrown off. Now, momentarily blinded by the light and the following darkness as MacAdoo, taking the other torch, rushed from the cave, Ruff lurched to his feet and ran after the big man.

Bursting from the small cavern, he saw the flickering of torchlight ahead of him, up a sloping passage which wound through great white pillars of limestone. The sound of water rushing past was in his ears, although he saw no water.

Ruff ran on, his blood pounding in his ears. The big man was quick and agile, more so than Ruff would have thought. He had gained much ground.

The trail ran up along the side of the cliff, winding capriciously. Ruff jogged on, Colt still in his hand. Where was Ginny? Where was Slaussen? He had to have heard those shots—it seemed the echoes were still reverberating through the massive cavern chambers.

Ruff was running through near-darkness now, the only light bleeding back to him from MacAdoo's torch. But he was gaining on the red-bearded Scotsman. He could hear his heavy breathing, the clomping of his boots against the stone.

Where was Slaussen?

The drop-off was more than fifty feet now, and the trail narrowing to an eyebrow. Still Ruff ran on wildly, his senses blind to fear and danger. An old feeling had uplifted him—it was a situation where a man had to kill or be killed, to be prepared to take a life or give his own up. A battle situation, and Ruff Justice had always been at his best at that moment when the bugle sounded, when the first shot resounded, when the wave of emotion which could make other men suffer dry-mouthed horror surged through a waiting army.

It was then that he felt he knew why he had been born at all—to fight, to meet the enemy hand to hand, to test his strength in the only meaningful way. To live or die.

MacAdoo's massive, bearded face gaped back across his shoulder. The man's face was crimson with beard and firelight and exertion. He turned, tried to run on, but Ruff lunged through space and caught his ankle.

MacAdoo spun furiously, clubbing at Ruff with the living torch, the head of it making angry hissing sounds as it arced out of the darkness.

Ruff clubbed at the back of MacAdoo's leg with his pistol, and the big man, bellowing in pain, went to his knee. The torch lay on the cold stone of the narrow path as MacAdoo dove at Ruff Justice, massive fists trying to reach Ruff, to pulverize his skull through sheer willpower.

He came close to doing it. The wild right MacAdoo threw glanced off Ruff's temple and then smashed into the stone beside Ruff's head. Ruff, himself on one knee, fired a left straight into MacAdoo's groin. There wasn't much point in wondering what the Marquess of Queensberry would have thought of that punch. It was effective, at least. MacAdoo sagged to his knees, bellowing and cursing. Ruff swung wildly with his Colt, slamming the barrel against the Scotsman's head.

It must have been made of iron. MacAdoo shrugged it off and barreled into Ruff, pawing at his face, trying to gouge his eyes with his thumbs. Ruff twisted his head frantically, hooked a hard left into MacAdoo's liver and another at his throat.

His head was close beside the fallen torch now, and Ruff could smell his own hair singeing, feel the heat of it against his face. MacAdoo grinned evilly. He got the idea.

He gripped Ruff by the hair and turned his face toward the flames. They licked at Justice as Ruff writhed and tried to free himself.

It was no good. There was too much strength in the big man's arms and hands. MacAdoo, his face bruised and scraped, drooled with anticipation as he inched Ruff's face nearer to the twisting yellow-and-red flames.

"They did say dead or alive," Ruff managed to pant. And then he shot him.

The Colt bucked against the palm of his hand and the .44 bullet punched into MacAdoo's body just below the lowest left-side rib. MacAdoo bellowed like a grizzly who has taken a big-bore slug and rolled away. He got to his feet, clutching his belly. Blood dripped from his lips, staining his beard to a darker red.

Ruff shot him again. The bullet lifted MacAdoo to his tiptoes, and he stood there for a minute, waving his arms frantically, trying to maintain his precarious balance before, with a pleasant nod, his eyes went vacant and he tumbled over the rim of the ledge and cartwheeled through the void below to land with a sickening thud on the stone floor of the cavern.

Ruff sat panting for a minute before he lifted himself to his feet, automatically shoving fresh loads into the cylinder of the .44 Colt.

Then, still panting, he picked up the torch with his left hand and started slowly up the trail.

Ahead there was a girl, a tender-eyed, tiny thing. And the man who liked to destroy women, who had raped them and killed them and given half a chance would do it again. Ruff didn't mean to give him half a chance.

He inched up the trail, knowing that Slaussen had heard the shots. The torch he carried was both a hazard and a necessity. He didn't mean to discard it until it had to be done. The path, extremely narrow, wound back on itself. It wasn't the sort of trail a man walked in darkness—not unless he wanted to end up where Mac-Adoo was, in much the same condition.

But there was no way back. No way to walk away from this even if he wanted to, and Ruff didn't. He wanted to see Slaussen go down before his gun, wanted to see him left to rot in this infernal cave, this Honeycomb Hades.

The first shot rang out as Ruff rounded the bend in the trail, and he went down, flinging the torch aside to hiss through the void.

Ruff lay still, his heart pounding. A second shot fired from an alcove ahead showed as a crimson muzzle flash, then as blue flame where the bullet ricocheted off the granite beside Ruff's hand.

"Justice!" It was Slaussen's voice, and Ruff's lip curled back. "Justice, I've got the girl."

Ruff crept ahead. He had the girl, and she was in trouble either way. He didn't want Ginny hurt, but he had no idea that backing away from Slaussen would ensure that she would survive. The man had proved otherwise.

"Justice? You hear me?"

Ruff heard him, heard the edge of panic in his voice. And he heard the barrage of singing bullets which flew wildly about the cavern, peppering Ruff with fragments of stone.

"I'll kill her!" Slaussen screamed, and his voice verged on being hysterical. A second voice interrupted Slaussen's warnings.

"Don't worry about me, Ruff! Get him, get the—!"

There was a savage sound, flesh on flesh, and the

voice—Ginny's voice, quavering, high-pitched—fell silent.

"Justice!"

Ruff didn't answer. He was still creeping his way upward, feeling his way along the ledge. His hair was in his eyes. MacAdoo's blood stained his hands. His knees and elbows were torn. But he would not stop, would not answer. Each movement was made with infinite care. His booted foot hitched forward a few inches, his hands sliding across the stone.

He knew what Slaussen was thinking now: Perhaps he had gotten Justice. Perhaps the man was already dead. Maybe he had won. His heart would lift with these hopes only to slow sullenly with doubt.

There was no light in all the world except for the dully glowing beams escaping from the cubbyhole where Slaussen hid. There was no sound but for that of running water as the underground river which wound through the cavern and surfaced briefly in that alcove burbled past, seeking an outlet.

"Justice!" The voice was a scream; the shots flew everywhere through the night, their roar incredible, the following whine of ricochets chilling. Smoke drifted across the void, acrid, pungent. Justice, pressing himself to the side of the cliff face, did not move.

"I know you're still there!"

He knew nothing of the sort, but Ruff didn't answer to prove the accuracy of the statement. He simply crept onward, inches at a time, the deadly Colt clutched in his scraped and battered hand.

He was near to the alcove entrance now, very near. He could even hear Tug Slaussen's asthmatic breathing. What he did not know was the situation inside the alcove. Did Slaussen have his gun against Ginny's head? Was there perhaps another nook where Slaussen could retreat to pot-shoot anyone entering the cave?

He didn't know, had no way of finding out—and it was time to make a decision. He had to rush Slaussen. There was no other way. Truthfully Ruff didn't want it any other way. He wanted it face to face, hard and fast.

Just now he had a problem. He was pinned down. Ginny was in there. Slaussen knew the cave as Ruff didn't. There had to be some way to shift the odds just a little.

He thought he had an idea, although he didn't like it much. If it worked it would at least give Ruff the edge of surprise. If it failed—well, the long ride, the dark nights, the battles would all be over.

Ruff reached back and tucked his Colt behind his belt. Then, eyes fixed on the faint glow ahead of him, he rolled to the edge of the trail and dropped over the rim.

He worked his way along the edge of the path, hands inching forward. Only his fingertips would be visible to anyone above, and it was unlikely that Slaussen would pick them up in the darkness. The greater risk by far was that this ape-stunting would plunge him a hundred feet toward the dark stone below.

Still, Ruff could think of no other way. This, if it worked, would allow him to see into the cavern, hide him from Slaussen's eyes, give him the advantage, however slight, of surprise.

His right hand slipped as he shifted it, and Ruff desperately clawed out. A handful of crumbling stone came free and he had to try again.

He hung there, his forehead pressed to the cold, rough stone, his pulse racing, silent curses twisting his lips. Then, taking a deep, slow breath, he went ahead.

Only occasionally he found a place to rest his boot toe, to just for a moment take the weight from his arms, which were knotted. It felt as if they would pull out at the shoulders, but he forced himself to hang on, to cling to the edge of the trail, to creep upward with the occasional wild cries of Slaussen ringing in his ears.

"Justice! Damn you, Justice!"

Then the shots, volleys of them singing through the cavern, the thunder of gunpowder rattling Ruff's eardrums. Then the silence, the slow creeping, clinging to the edge of that crumbled trail, his boots dangling in the bottomless void at his feet.

Sweat trickled into Ruff's burning eyes. His fingers were cramped and wooden. How near was he? Could he take the chance of peering over the rim? Not yet. Not yet, he didn't think.

The ideal time would seem to be after Slaussen had fired still another of his hateful lead barrages, when he would presumably step back into the light of the cavern to reload, when his defenses might be down just for a fraction of a minute. Maybe. Guessing wrong could get a man killed.

He knew it would have to be soon, however; his grip was beginning to fail. The demand he was placing on his arms was debilitating. When he had to make his move, if he took too long deciding, those muscles would be next to useless.

Slaussen made the decision for him.

"Justice!" There was a note of madness in Slaussen's voice now.

The bullets rang through the cavern yet again as the harried outlaw emptied his gun. He was still firing down the trail, Ruff noted with grim satisfaction. Slaussen had no idea where his adversary was.

Ruff waited until the echoes died away. Then, cautiously, he pulled himself up. It was time. The time to live . . . or to die.

15

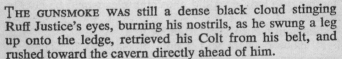

THE GUNSMOKE WAS still a dense black cloud stinging Ruff Justice's eyes, burning his nostrils, as he swung a leg up onto the ledge, retrieved his Colt from his belt, and rushed toward the cavern directly ahead of him.

He had hoped to find Slaussen with an empty gun, but it wasn't to be. In fact, as Ruff's eyes discovered, sweeping the room in the instant before the guns blazed, Slaussen had had three rifles against the stone wall of the alcove near the entrance.

All of them were out of his reach just now, but the revolver in his hand was cocked and ready, and it stabbed flame as Ruff burst into the stony alcove.

Ruff felt a searing burn, like a branding iron placed along the side of his neck, felt himself tugged to one side, half spun around, even as Slaussen, his face a mask of fury, triggered off again.

Ruff dove toward the floor of the cavern, moving to his left, keeping his right arm, his gun arm, clear. He fired twice in rapid succession as he fell, saw Tug Slaussen jolted back, saw Slaussen's pistol fired into the floor, a red-hot ricochet shearing off harmlessly.

Ruff had been making his plans even as he hurled himself to the earth. He had seen the crates to one side, seen the Wells Fargo box, long since emptied, among them. He had seen Ginny, sitting on the floor, holding her cheek, her hair around her face, her eyes wide with the bloody spectacle of this day.

Ruff dove behind the boxes, firing again as Slaussen, recovering himself, splintered the crates with searching bullets. Ruff was temporarily out of sight but hardly out of danger. The .44s tore the boxes to kindling as Justice smoothly, rapidly reloaded his smoking Colt.

Ruff closed the loading gate, lay back, head against the cold stone floor, counted three, and came up firing. He winged two shots at the darting Slaussen, saw him crumple up as one shot hit home, crippling a leg, saw the distorted, animal expression on Slaussen's face.

Ruff started to pop off yet another shot and suddenly had to hold up, his muzzle veering away, up and to the right. Slaussen, sliding, stumbling, had reached Ginny. Yanking her to her feet, he backed away, the blue pistol in his hand at her head.

Slaussen was leaving a smeared trail of blood across the floor of the cavern, but it didn't seem to be slowing him down just now.

Ruff could only stand and watch, his pistol ready for a chance shot as Slaussen, still raving, screaming, backed away, the muzzle of his revolver against the petrified Ginny's head.

"So damn tough! Couldn't let it go. Couldn't forget that Indian squaw. What was it to you?" Slaussen continued to drag Ginny backward, his forearm across her throat. "That other woman didn't have to die—I was aiming for you. You know that. I was aiming for you because I knew you wouldn't quit. I knew you'd hunt me till you found me. I had to try for you first! Damn it all, Justice . . . if only you'da learned to quit!"

Then he was gone. Gone! Both Slaussen and Ginny vanishing into nowhere. The splash followed, and Ruff crossed the room at a run.

The underground river, always audible but always invisible, flowed darkly past. There was a three-foot bank and then nothing but black, quickly running water. That and Tug Slaussen.

He still had Ginny by the neck, and he was dragging her down. She struggled, kicked out, twisted in his grip, all to no avail.

Ruff teetered on the edge of the stone bank for a single moment, saw Slaussen lift his weapon and fire. There was no report as the waterlogged cartridge refused to answer the primer's muffled hissing urge.

Ruff's eyes flickered downstream, and he saw with panic that the river running through this honeycombed deathtrap was swallowed up by solid stone once again.

The black water ran underground, vanishing after passing through this grotto—and Slaussen, wild-eyed, laughing and sputtering, was taking Ginny with him along this underground river.

Ruff dove toward them. Ahead he saw Slaussen's head, saw Ginny try to claw his eyes, saw the black river rush on, flowing downward into the heart of the cavern once more. Ruff took a deep breath, stretched out a long arm, and caught Slaussen by the collar. Then, with a swirling, hammering surge, the bottom dropped out.

The river, black as ink, angry and tumbling, fell straight downward, blustering through the stony caverns, and Ruff Justice fell with the irresistible current, still clinging to Tug Slaussen.

He hammered away at Slaussen's body even as they were twisted around and torn by the sucking currents, and as blow after blow—padded by the mass of water, but not enough for Slaussen's good—struck home, Ruff felt the air go out of Slaussen's body, felt him grappling for life, straining to surface . . . except there was no surface. There was no oxygen.

They fell in a twisted, struggling tangle through liquid black hell. And then suddenly Slaussen was struggling no more. Ruff felt him go slack, and he released his grip.

Justice was brought up hard against a projection. His lungs were on fire, pleading for oxygen; but the river, rushing on along its underground course, was merciless.

It clawed at him, compressed his lungs, turned the

lights of desperation on in his skull, caused a thousand crazy images to spring to the forefront of his oxygen-starved brain.

He was slammed against hard, unyielding stone again and again, turned end for end, and still it was not ended. It was over—Ruff knew it suddenly. It was over and he was a dead man. This was the nightmare preceding death. He was not meant to ever see light again. Some malignant cave spirit had taken him and crushed the life from him.

He had time to wonder about Ginny. Had she managed to avoid being pulled under by this implacable black river, or was she too . . . ?

Ruff surged toward it before he had time to think, to consciously recommend to his battered body a course of action. It was instinct and only instinct, the hunger of an organism for survival.

It wasn't much at first—a faint promise, a bluish hope. Then he knew. Knew it was the surface of the river, that the river had emerged once more from its underground source, and he fought to find the surface with the last of his strength.

The bluish light became paler, more brilliant. He wasn't going to make it, knew he wasn't, and then his arm, struggling to pull him upward, broke the surface and Ruff came up, his deprived lungs sucking in water with the air.

Choking, coughing, he let his eyes be pierced by the dazzling sunlight. The burning in his lungs slowly diminished, the choking coughs finally subsided, and Ruff could breathe, actually breathe and see!

He was floating on his back down a peaceful river overhung by willow trees. Cicadas sang in the brush along the shore. The sun was a brilliant yellow ball floating in a high, cloudless sky.

He didn't make any attempt to swim for the sandy bluff along the river's edge. Not just yet. He savored the flowing in and out of breath, felt the sunlight against his face, the slowing current of the river as it broadened.

And then he saw something which put new strength in his body, which drew him to the shore like a magnet. Ginny! Sitting exhausted but smiling on the shore beneath a sandy bluff where the mottled shade of cottonwoods fell. The light danced in her eyes and on her damp hair as she stood and came to him.

Ruff waded from the river, his buckskins sodden and heavy.

"Ruff." It was all she said, and then she held him, kissing him on cheek and chin, nose and mouth, beaming up at him when she was done, her hands touching his arms and shoulders with amazement.

"I didn't think . . ." she began, but Ruff quieted her with a long, deep kiss. The sun was warm on his shoulders; she was warm in his arms.

"Look at it," Ruff said, lifting his eyes to the long-running sky. "It's a dreamer's world."

"And a lover's," Ginny suggested.

"Who's more a dreamer?" Ruff answered.

"I can't believe it's over," she said. "I can't believe . . ." And then she put her hands to her mouth, drawing away from Ruff sharply.

"What is it?" he asked, but she could only lift a finger. Following it, Ruff's eyes saw the thing floating downstream.

The thing, slowly bobbing, face down, lifeless. It was Tug Slaussen, and Ruff watched in fascination as Tug, or what had been Tug, bumped up against a snag and remained motionless, suspended on the river's surface. He could stay there until the fish had pared the flesh from his bones, until those bones sank to the surface of the slowly rambling river and were buried in the silty bottom.

"Come on," Ruff said, grinning at the woman beside him, the small, bright-eyed woman who could not erase Louise's memory, but who could soften the sorrow and for a time at least share his life.

They plodded up the low bluff together, Ginny leaning on him a little—her ankle was still sore. The sun was warm, the day bright. It was like being reborn, Ruff decided. Dying in that black cavern, being pulled under by a black river . . .

He stopped abruptly, his arm tightening around Ginny's shoulder.

"What is it?" she asked, her eyes sparkling, amused. Then she too looked ahead, and the pleasure fell away from her face. A bare-chested Sioux, rifle in hand, wearing paint and war bonnet, stood atop the bluff glaring down at them.

To be reborn to die once more. Ruff didn't even have a gun. He could only watch as the Sioux lifted the rifle to his shoulder and aimed.

Ginny clung to him. Ruff squeezed her again. Then, inexplicably, the rifle was lowered and the Sioux was gone. They heard hoofbeats a moment later, and when Ginny looked her question at Ruff he could only shrug.

The answer lay at the crest of the bluff. From there, looking out onto the flats, the long line of blue-clad cavalry was clearly visible. The Sioux hadn't wanted to announce his presence to such a body of men.

And there were many of them. Strung out across the plains, approaching through the shimmering veils of rising heat as Ruff and Ginny staggered toward them.

Reaching the road they were traveling, they stood and waited, Ruff's arm around the tiny blue-eyed woman. The soldiers came on, Colonel MacEnroe himself at their head. When he saw Ruff Justice standing before his patrol, his long dark hair drifting in the breeze, a young, quite pretty woman with him, MacEnroe wiped his eyes with the back of his gloved hand as if he were seeing the impossible.

MacEnroe halted his party, drawing his big bay gelding up directly before Ruff.

"Damn you, you rascal!" MacEnroe said. But his eyes twinkled as he said it. "What in hell are you doing out here, Justice?"

"Picnic, sir," Ruff said, straight-faced.

"I've had men out looking for you. Why aren't you ever around when I need you?" MacEnroe blustered.

"The order, sir."

"The order—oh, that one. Well, damn that order! We've need of a scout. In case you haven't heard, there's a thousand Sioux just north of here—"

"South, sir," Ruff interrupted.

"Eh?" MacEnroe frowned.

"Their main camp is south."

"But rumors drifting into Lincoln—"

"Well, sir, rumors are all fine and good, but I've seen them," Ruff said, the beginnings of a grin tugging at the corners of his mouth.

"Seen 'em!" MacEnroe blustered. "Major Burnett, Ruff Justice has seen the camp and he says it's south."

"Yes, sir," Burnett said patiently, "I'm sure, but our informants—"

"Dammit, major, this is *Ruff Justice*. Best damned scout on the plains. Always has been." He turned sharply on the major. "Why didn't you sign him up when he was at Lincoln, by the way? Gross negligence that."

"Sir, the order was—"

"The order again! Why does everyone keep throwing that damned *persona non grata* order in my face? How in the devil, sir, do you *ever* expect to make light colonel if you've got to quibble over every little point? Learn to make decisions, man!"

The major muttered something and shook his head in confusion. MacEnroe again spoke to Ruff: "We're riding. South. Don't suppose you'd care to lead us, Ruff?"

"Not this time, sir." Ginny turned her eyes down as Ruff squeezed her shoulder again. "Not just now. But if you'd lend us some provisions and horses, I'd appreciate it."

"I understand, boy." MacEnroe jabbed a finger at him. "But you show up again at Lincoln, hear me? We've got to get you back on the rolls. Sergeant, cut out two spare horses for Justice." Turning his head, he lifted an arm, gave the command "for'ard," and touching the brim of his hat to Ginny, he led his force out southward.

Ginny never saw the colonel's gesture. She was aware of nothing, of no one but the strong man who held her in his arms and kissed her as the columns of cavalry horses passed them by, their dust sifting past, becoming bright gold in the brilliant sunlight of the Dakota morning.

JOIN THE <u>RUFF JUSTICE</u> READER'S PANEL
AND PREVIEW NEW BOOKS

If you're a reader of <u>RUFF JUSTICE</u>, New American Library wants to bring you more of the type of books you enjoy. For this reason we're asking you to join <u>RUFF JUSTICE</u> Reader's Panel, to preview new books, so we can learn more about your reading tastes.

Please fill out and mail today. Your comments are appreciated.

1. The title of the last paperback book I bought was: _____
_____

2. How many paperback books have you bought for yourself in the last six months?
☐ 1 to 3   ☐ 4 to 6   ☐ 10 to 20   ☐ 21 or more

3. What other paperback fiction have you read in the past six months? Please list titles: _____
_____
_____

4. I usually buy my books at: (Check One or more)
☐ Book Store   ☐ Newsstand   ☐ Discount Store
☐ Supermarket   ☐ Drug Store   ☐ Department Store
☐ Other (Please specify) _____

5. I listen to radio regularly: (Check One)   ☐ Yes   ☐ No
My favorite station is: _____
I usually listen to radio (Circle One or more)   On way to work /
During the day / Coming home from work / In the evening

6. I read magazines regularly: (Check One)   ☐ Yes   ☐ No
My favorite magazine is: _____

7. I read a newspaper regularly: (Check One)   ☐ Yes   ☐ No
My favorite newspaper is: _____
My favorite section of the newspaper is: _____

For our records, we need this information from all our Reader's Panel Members.
NAME: _____
ADDRESS: _____ ZIP _____
TELEPHONE: Area Code ( ) Number _____

8. (Check One)   ☐ Male   ☐ Female

9. Age (Check One)   ☐ 17 and under   ☐ 18 to 34
☐ 35 to 49   ☐ 50 to 64   ☐ 65 and over

10. Education (Check One)
☐ Now in high school   ☐ Graduated high school
☐ Now in college   ☐ Completed some college
☐ Graduated college

As our special thanks to all members of our Reader's Panel, we'll send a free gift of special interest to readers of <u>RUFF JUSTICE</u>.

Thank you. Please mail this in today.

NEW AMERICAN LIBRARY
PROMOTION DEPARTMENT
1633 BROADWAY
NEW YORK, NY 10019